Valynn

Book Two in
The Andley Sisters Series

Sherri Beth Johnson

DEDICATION

In memory of my sweet friends....

Kimberly (Kimmy) Lynne Misener Stephens
May 15, 1973 – March 2, 2006

And

Beth Ann Bertschy Austin
August 16, 1973 – December 19, 2013

*I love and miss you both,
and I will always treasure our memories.*

Other Books By Sherri Beth Johnson

The Andley Sisters Series, Farmers Daughters

Georgiana, Book One

Valynn, Book Two

Genevieve, Book Three

Augusta, Book Four

The Kenrick Brides Series

Charleigh, Book One

The Royals of Gliston Series

Estelle, Book One

Taisia, Book Two

Anne of Fales, Book Three

Gracelyn, Book Four

Cairistiona, Book Five

Gemma, Book Six

CONTENTS

ACKNOWLEDGMENTS

I first want to thank my Heavenly Father and Jesus Christ for gifting me this book series. I want to thank my family for supporting me and for putting up with me and my anxiety as we launched the release of *Georgiana*. I want to thank my editor and dear friend Lora for her hard work and support. I want to thank my mother, mother-in-law, and my sweet friend Ramona for being my cheerleaders. For my beautiful daughter Victoria, thank you ,for being my inspiration and sounding board. And to my little miracle man Zane, you inspire me to never give up, for it is through your life that I have been led to dig deeply within myself. And last, but not least, I want to thank my husband Jared for choosing me, believing in me, being my forever love story, and for holding my hand on this wild ride we call life. I adore you!

Prologue

I sat in stunned silence, staring back at the grey eyes that had become so familiar to me over the last year. I swallowed hard and struggled for my next breath.

"Valynn, I will return in six months or so. It isn't as if I am leaving forever," I heard him say.

Forever, he had said *forever*, but not in the context I had been expecting. I sat here, on my sister Georgiana's front porch, the evening of my eighteenth birthday with the man I had assumed I would marry, *my* Isaac Stein. Isaac, with his playful grey eyes I had come to adore and dark hair. Isaac, my childhood friend. Isaac, the man who had courted me for the past year. He was leaving, and he asked me to wait for him.

"Isaac, I do not think waiting will do any good," I admitted softly. I had to be honest; I had felt for some months the same restlessness he presented tonight. I told myself he was happy, just anxious to be married, but in truth, I had to admit I had felt this coming. Perhaps I had even hoped this night would come.

"What do you mean, Valynn? Of course waiting will work. In six months, perhaps seven, I will return with a pile of gold and be ready to settle down," he said, gently taking my hand in his.

His touch felt so familiar, so safe, but perhaps too familiar and too safe. Our eyes met, and I shook my head no. "Isaac, I release you from our courtship. We both know I have been of age to marry now for a year. If you truly wanted to marry me, you would have," I sighed.

He shook his head. "There is only you, Valynn; you are the only woman I will ever love. I am just asking for more time. I can't explain it, but I have to go. I have to see for myself the hills filled with gold. I am no good here until I get this out of my system. But I *will* return, and for *you*, Valynn. *I love you*," he insisted.

I pulled my hand away and stood looking out over Kenrick Farms. I heard my brother-in-law Keane inside laughing at something my sister Georgiana said about their new baby Jori. "Do you hear that, Isaac?" I asked softly.

Isaac smiled and stood beside me.

"*That* is true love. Keane will not leave my sister's side for more than half a day," I said, wanting a love like Georgie had found.

"It didn't start out that way," Isaac reminded me.

I nodded in agreement. It had not started out well for Georgie, not at all. But she had persevered and was now deeply loved.

"Perhaps it isn't just you running away, Isaac. Perhaps I am concerned as well. If I truly loved you, I would wait, no matter how long," I said, searching my heart.

Isaac pulled me closely to him. "I know you love me, Valynn," he insisted.

My eyes filled with tears as they met his. "Not enough to wait. I have waited a year. I will not wait any longer," I said decisively.

"So this is it? You are breaking it off with me, after all this time?" he asked, as if it had never been done in the history of courtships, and I knew it had never been done to him.

"Yes, I am. I will always think of you fondly, Isaac. We have had a lot of good times this past year," I said, wiping a tear from my eye, but feeling strongly that God was leading me through a new door.

At least I prayed I was deciphering God correctly. I was often known to rush things, and I prayed my restlessness was the start of something new that God had for me. I had expected Isaac to propose tonight. His telling me that he was leaving on a wild goose chase looking for gold was confirmation that my restlessness of the past few months was for a reason.

"That we have, Valynn, and I do not want to lose you. Why can't I have my dreams and my girl at the same time?" he asked, pressing his forehead against mine tenderly.

"You will someday… when it is right," I whispered.

"But *you* feel right to me," he pleaded.

I sighed heavily; this was harder than I had imagined, and yet I knew it was for the best.

"Happy birthday, Valynn. I am sorry, but I cannot wish you love and blessings. I can only wish you to wait for me," he said, kissing my forehead softly.

I watched him leave my party with a heavy heart. He must have turned to look back at me three times before he made it to his horse that was tied up out by the oak tree. When his trail was merely dust, I felt a warm arm come around my shoulders, and I smiled weakly as my sister Georgiana hugged me closely.

"No proposal tonight?" she asked softly.

I shook my head no. "There will not be one. I told him I will not wait any longer. I released him from our courtship," I said, sighing.

"Oh Val, I am sorry," Georgie said tenderly.

I shook my head no. "I am actually all right. I mean, a part of me feels heartbroken, but I think I have known for a while that it wasn't going to happen. I think I will be all right," I said, deciding right there and then that I meant it. *I was going to be just fine.*

CHAPTER ONE

It had been three months since Isaac had left in search of gold. I had not heard a single word from him. January was nearly over, and I found my heart had healed quite nicely. "Oh, it's all right, Jori, it's all right," I said, bouncing the fussy infant in my arms and loving the sweet baby scent of her hair against my cheek. "I think you are hungry. Let us go find your momma," I said, wrapping my niece warmly in her little bunting bag Georgie had made for her and heading towards the barn.

I knew Keane and Georgiana had a meeting with Dr. McCray, the town's first veterinarian, and I prayed it was nearly over for little Jori would wait no longer. My stomach fluttered nervously at seeing the handsome doctor again. I had only seen him in church on Sundays since the day Jori had been born three months ago, and he had never looked my way. I chuckled to myself that he was a bit old for me, but something about him gave me butterflies.

I walked into the barn, and Georgiana winced. "I am so sorry, Valynn; I knew it was getting to be time. You remember Dr. McCray from the day Ophelia and Jori were born, don't you?" she asked, knowing I had causally asked about him a few times when we cooked together in the kitchen.

"Yes of course, Dr. McCray, it is good to see you again," I said, bouncing the fussy baby.

To my surprise Dr. McCray walked up to me and smiled, his teeth so white, his skin so tan, his eyes the deepest green. "It is nice to see you again, Miss Andley. And you as well, Miss Jori Kenrick," he said, bending over to smile at the baby. Jori let out a screech. She was beyond bouncing now. "Oh my, I didn't mean to upset her," Dr. McCray chuckled nervously as he backed away.

I blushed and was thankful when Georgie took the baby and headed to the house to feed her. Henry called for Keane, and he quickly excused himself leaving Dr. McCray and me alone.

"So, how did Ophelia check out?" I asked, surprised at how nervous I found myself. I was not usually prone to nerves.

Dr. McCray smiled brightly. I could tell he loved his job. "Perfectly! She is a beauty. I enjoy coming to Kenrick Farms and working with the Percherons," he said, starting to pack up his bag.

I nodded. "They are beautiful animals," I agreed, not knowing what else to say.

"I was out at the Stein farm yesterday. It seems like there will be several new Arabian foals in a few months. You must be excited," he said, turning back to me.

I blushed. "I didn't know. Isaac never spoke much about the farm. He has left to search for gold," I said, wanting to say more, such as, *I am free to pursue you now*. But of course, I didn't. I was always saying things I shouldn't, my sisters said, so I refrained.

Dr. McCray raised an eyebrow. "Gold huh, and you are good with this?" he asked, surprised.

I couldn't help but smile. "No, I wasn't all right with his decision. We have parted ways, mutually," I said but then remembered poor Isaac had asked me to wait, expected me to wait, and had been devastated when I had broken things off with him. Did I dare to hope that was a spark of interest I now saw in Dr. McCray's beautiful green eyes?

"Oh, forgive me; I should not have mentioned it. I knew, of course, you were courting Isaac. I had not heard that it had ended. I am sorry," he stammered.

"It is all right. Isaac and I have been friends most of our lives. I suppose that is what we were meant to be. I find myself relieved and doing just fine," I said, smiling to ensure him I meant what I said.

"Good, that is good," he said, smiling brightly.

Keane returned, and I bid Dr. McCray a good day, knowing he would be leaving any minute. I was walking back towards the house, his beautiful green eyes branded before my eyes, when I heard him call to me.

"Miss Andley! Wait, Miss Andley!"

I quickly turned. "Yes, Dr. McCray?" I asked, giving him my best smile with my heart racing.

"I was just going to ask...if you would be interested in going for a buggy ride with me after church on Sunday?" he asked awkwardly.

I shivered and smiled. It was awfully cold for a buggy ride, but of course, I wouldn't turn him down. "Of course! I would be delighted. Thank you for asking." I would simply wear multiple layers of flannel underwear beneath my skirts, *anything* for a chance to get to know him better.

"Excellent. I will see you Sunday then," he said, nodding.

My heart raced at his handsomeness. "Sunday," I agreed and turned to run into the house.

I walked into the warm kitchen were Georgie nursed Jori, and Mormor sat at the table with her tea. I squealed with delight, nearly causing Mormor to drop her teacup and Jori to turn and look at me, near to cry.

"Valynn!" Georgie scolded.

I quickly apologized but knew my cheeks were red with delight, not just cold. "He just asked me for a buggy ride," I said breathlessly, sitting as calmly as I could at the table.

"Oh, what, wait, who?" Georgie asked excitedly.

"Dr. McCray, this Sunday!" I said, hardly able to contain myself.

"Oh, mercy Valynn! Are you certain? I mean, he is a little older than you, maybe six or seven years I would think," Georgie said, concerned.

I waved her concern away with my hand. "I do not care about that. Anything under twelve years of age difference is acceptable. Besides, I think I may find a more mature man is what I need," I assured her, thinking of Isaac and his immaturity and inability to commit.

My sister smiled. "Niall McCray is a nice man, and he does have a good job. You would be well provided for, and Father would be ecstatic to have a veterinarian in the family," Georgie said, smiling. I smiled and bobbed my head in agreement.

"Who would ask for a buggy ride in the freezing winter?" Mormor complained.

I shrugged. "Perhaps he wants to snuggle me close," I said, bursting into laughter. I quickly apologized when I saw her disapproval. "I need to run on home now before it gets dark. But I will come again to help tomorrow afternoon," I said, kissing my sister's cheek goodbye and the top of Jori's sweet little head.

I rode my father's mare home quickly. I could hardly wait to tell my mother and younger sisters. Genevieve would be so jealous.

The next morning I rode with my father into town to get a few supplies before the next snowfall. I couldn't help but hope I would run into Dr. McCray. He had a small office on the edge of town next to a large brick house where he lived.

"Sit still, Valynn! You would think you were no more than five years old the way you are acting," my father chuckled.

I smiled brightly. Father had indeed been excited that Dr. McCray had asked me on a buggy ride for the coming Sunday. I wanted to look at the fabrics in the mercantile and perhaps sew a new dress for the occasion, thus I had begged my father to allow me to accompany him despite the cold day.

He left me at the mercantile to purchase the supplies as he went down to the feed store, promising to return in half an hour.

"Good morning, Mrs. Larkin," I greeted as I sailed into the mercantile and headed straight back to the fabrics.

"Good morning, Valynn. How is your mother?" she asked, joining me.

"She is well, thank you for asking," I answered, lifting a nice tan and black plaid for a better look.

"Looks like you're going to make a dress. Look at this one; it just came in this week," she said, leading me to a soft pink, grey and black plaid flannel.

"Oh, how lovely! Yes, this is it. This is perfect," I said, smiling. I chose black velvet to trim the neckline, sleeves, and skirt and then tiny black satin buttons.

Mrs. Larkin cut the fabrics for me and then went to fill the list my mother had sent. I browsed the aisles as I waited, humming to myself and picturing my new dress and how I would look in my pink flannel against the setting of a pale and wintery sky.

Just then I looked up, only to see Dr. McCray walking by. My heart raced, but soon I saw he wasn't alone. He was walking with Ava Stein, Isaac's sister, who was five years my senior.

My heart sank to the floor as Mrs. Larkin called me to the front. "Here is everything on your list, Valynn. Tell your mother I said hello," she said, smiling.

I thanked her, quickly paid her the money I owed, looked down the street to where Dr. McCray had just passed, and saw them walking into the diner together. His arm linked with hers. Ava Stein, the woman who would have been my sister-in-law if I had married Isaac.

I looked to see my father heading my way in his buggy, and I quickly helped him load our supplies. My heart was heavy and my temper furious. How could Dr. McCray have asked me for a buggy ride just yesterday and then be with Ava at the diner today?

"How about I treat my girl to a hot lunch before we head home?" my father said, smiling.

I gasped, of all the days for my father to want to treat me. "Oh, no! I am not hungry," I said quickly.

He raised an eyebrow. "You are always hungry, Valynn."

And he had me there; I was always hungry, but not today, not now. "It looks like snow any minute, we should hurry home," I suggested.

Father shook his head. "No, I am cold and need a hot cup of coffee, and at least a piece of pie, to hold me over until we get home. Come, Daughter, join your old papa."

I smiled weakly.

I allowed Father to escort me into the diner, and my face turned crimson as soon as I saw them sitting together. To my shock, and horror, Dr. McCray gave me a friendly little wave and a handsome smile.

I raised my chin a little higher and flashed him my best smile but prayed the daggers shooting from my eyes hit their mark.

"Of all the nerve!" I thought silently. I had just caught him with another woman, and he was acting as if nothing had happened at all, even flirting with me in front of her with his little wave and flashy smile.

My father looked shocked to see Ava and Dr. McCray together but greeted them both civilly as we took our seats at a small table across the room, far across the room to where I had quickly led him.

Once we were settled and had ordered our dinner, my father took my hand tenderly. "I am sorry, my Val. I didn't know. This is why you were not hungry?" he softly asked me.

I nodded. I was so mad at that no-good-horse-doctoring-Romeo.

"He must be playing the field around a little which, honestly, is wise. You yourself should get to know more young men. You were tied to Isaac for a year. Now it is time to get to know a few more young fellows. Makes deciding easier," Father said, sipping his coffee.

I merely nodded. I hated to admit that it stung my pride to see Dr. McCray with another woman, for I truly did feel flutters when I was around him. had lain awake most of the night thinking of a possible future with the handsome doctor. It irritated me to no end that I found him so attractive and intriguing.

I cast a glance their way to find them deep in conversation, oblivious that I was in the room. I sighed, hating to admit to myself that Ava was more likely suited for him. Ava had always attended a private girl's school up North. The Steins were quite wealthy, and with Ava being the only daughter, they wanted her skilled in all the fine arts and languages. She was the image of social grace and dignity; although her face was rather plain, she held herself elegantly and it helped her to be attractive.

I was a simple farm girl. Yes, I loved to dress up and go to dances or dinner parties, but the next day you would find me mucking out stalls and milking cows or working in the garden.

Ava had never stepped foot in a barn I was certain. It hurt to think of it, but Dr. McCray would find conversation with Ava more to his liking as they had both attended college, and I had only went to the eighth grade as most girls in our small farming community.

I decided then and there, I had to get over this infatuation with Dr. McCray and his beautiful green eyes.

When we returned home, I put on my riding skirt and bundled up warmly. Taking my new fabrics, I rode over to Kenrick Farms to see Georgie. She would know how to make this better. I would laugh with her, love on my sweet niece, and soon forget my heartache which had now turned completely into anger towards the handsome veterinarian.

Mormor greeted me at the kitchen door, and soon I was sitting at the table with her and Georgie over a cup of hot cocoa, relaying what had happened that morning.

Georgie's angry face was too funny and I had to laugh. She could have a temper at times, and seeing me in distress was quickly bringing it to surface.

"Well, I knew no good would come of a man asking for a buggy ride in this cold. That shows you his intentions were not where they should be, and now he has another girl on the side. You would do good to forget him, Valynn," Mormor warned.

"Surely he will not expect you to take a ride with him now that you have caught him with Ava?" Georgie asked, outraged.

I shrugged. "We are forgetting he is a free man; he could be seeing several women in town. Papa said it is called playing the field around, and that it is wise," I said, sighing, not agreeing with my father in the least.

"Well, then you too will play this field around and see several different men in town. Didn't Ben Weston, Drew's brother, ask you to dance a few weeks ago at the Smythe's party?" Georgie asked me.

I nodded and sighed heavily. Although Ben Weston had always been somewhat of a pain in my backside growing up, I had to admit he had turned out quite handsome.

"What we need is another party, another dance to show the men in town you are truly free of your courtship with

Isaac. And, to show Dr. Niall McCray that there are other men vying for your attentions," Georgie said decisively.

"But there aren't any other parties that I know of," I said in defeat.

"Well, then, we shall plan one ourselves here at Kenrick Farms. I know, a Valentine's dance! It is only two weeks away. You will have to help me, Valynn. We will of course get Genevieve and Augusta to watch Jori for me. We will announce it at church this Sunday. Oops, I suppose I had best ask Keane first," Georgie giggled.

Mormor offered her services to help, and we sat at the table for an hour planning the event. Then Mormor and I retired to the parlor to start sewing my new dress, which I would now save for the dance, since Dr. McCray would no doubt back out of our buggy ride.

The rest of the week went by quickly as I traveled to Kenrick Farms daily to work on my dress and help Georgie plan the Valentine dance.

I hurried this day, Saturday, because the weather looked ominous of snow, and I would be needed back home. As I swung off my horse, I was startled when warm hands caught my waist. I squealed in surprise as a man lifted me effortlessly down to the ground. I whirled around to find the handsome Dr. McCray smiling mischievously.

"I am sorry, Miss Andley; I did not mean to frighten you," he said, causing me to blush as I stared into his handsome face.

Why did he have to be so beautiful? "Thank you for scaring ten years off my life, Dr. McCray. I suppose I didn't need them much," I said, blushing and smiling in return.

He grinned. "I am afraid the weather looks to bring snow soon. We may have to reschedule our buggy ride tomorrow," he sighed.

I raised my chin higher, surprised he still intended to take me. I wondered if this was his way of telling me he wished to take Ava instead. "Yes, perhaps that is best. It isn't really the season for buggy rides is it?" My anger was returning quickly. I tried my best to remember all the lectures I had received growing up, the ones specifically of my speaking before thinking and controlling my temper, but I found I was drawing blanks.

"I suppose it isn't. So, what activities do you suggest, Miss Andley, if a man wished to court a woman, and the weather was cold?" he asked me, smiling that handsome smile.

My heart raced. Had he just mentioned courting? Did he want to court me? I shrugged. "Why don't you just ask Ava? I am certain with all her schooling, she would have a right proper idea for you. Good day, Dr. McCray," I said, smiling coyly and walking toward the house.

"Wait, please, Miss Andley. Valynn? Wait!" he laughed and caught up to me.

I stopped and forced a smile.

"You are angry with me because of Miss Stein?" he asked, quite pleased with the situation it appeared. His green eyes shone brightly.

I sighed, *here it went.* I was always prone to speak my mind. "I am a little angry, I suppose, *and* perhaps a little hurt seeing you with her. But, now I have resigned myself to the fact that truly... you and Ava are more suited for one another than you and I. I have always liked Ava, and although it pained me at first, I have to agree with your choice." I left him once again for the house.

"Wait, Valynn! May I call you Valynn?" he asked breathlessly.

I turned my head to the side in thought. "I think Miss Andley would be best," I said, smiling as if he didn't affect me one bit.

He nodded, a little disappointed perhaps. "Miss Andley, do you think Mrs. Kenrick would allow us the use of her kitchen and perhaps a cup of coffee so we could talk?" he asked, seeming desperate to talk to me.

"I do not see that we have anything to talk about, Dr. McCray, but, Georgie is always welcoming. You look like you could use a warm up. Come along," I said, rather demanding.

He merely chuckled and followed me into the warm, cheery red and white kitchen.

Of course Georgie was thrilled that Dr. McCray was present and wanted time to speak with me. She quickly made tea and excused herself to her bedroom to sew while Jori napped.

I led Dr. McCray into the parlor and stoked the fire, then served the tea and cake Georgie had made.

"I love coming here to Kenrick Farms. It is a beautiful farm, and it feels like home," Dr. McCray surprised me by saying.

I smiled and couldn't help but want to know more about this aggravating man. "I assumed it was just for the Percherons," I said, knowing he was thrilled to be helping Keane with his new horse breeding business.

"Well, that too, of course. *And*, I always seem to run into *you* here," he added with a playful wink.

I found myself blushing and silently scolded myself not to fall into his trap of causing me to care more for him than I already did. "I, too, love it here. The house, *my* home that is, hasn't been the same since Georgie and Celia married. I find myself visiting here often," I confided.

"So, is that what you desire as well, Miss Andley- a farm, a home, a family?" he asked, surprising me.

I nodded. "Yes, it has always been my dream," I admitted.

He smiled as if this news pleased him.

"And what of you, Dr. McCray? You have served your time in your education and now stumbled into our small community. What are your plans?" I asked, pouring him another cup of tea.

He smiled and shook his head. "I am not for certain, but I assume the same as you. I closed on my farm last week. I now own it. I suppose a family comes next logically," he admitted.

I smiled, for this news pleased me as well. "You have chosen a lovely farm and have the best of both worlds. You have land, but it's not too close to town where you can still have peace." I had always admired the tall red brick house and farm on the outskirts of town. I could completely imagine myself living there.

"Yes! That is it exactly, Miss Andley. I need to be close to town for emergencies. But yet, I, too, want my own place of peace at the end of a work day," he said, thankful I understood.

We talked a bit more as he explained the work that needed to be done to the house, which was older but beautiful, in my opinion. I could almost feel myself living there, helping to transform the place.

Suddenly, he sat his cup down and leaned forward boldly. "So, you do not approve of me courting several women at one time do you?" he asked, throwing me off.

For once I sat stunned, unable to speak. I had honestly never heard of such a thing, it truly never happened here in my small community. A man asked a lady to court, they courted and either married or decided against marriage and went on to court another.

I decided I had to be honest. Unfortunately, that was always my downfall, speaking my mind. "I cannot help but think it unwise. *If* I were one of the women you were courting, then of course I would be jealous. Jealousy is such an ugly thing, in anyone, and I despise it. *But*, as an innocent bystander, I can honestly say, that it could possibly be an alternative way to narrowing down your options on who is best to marry," I said decisively, although my heart failed me, and for a moment, I felt like begging him to forget about Ava and marry me.

He smiled, taking my breath away. "You are very direct, Miss Andley," he said, lifting an eyebrow.

I blushed and nodded. "It is my downfall, I'm afraid. I am not one to be demure and play games. I have no patience for such things. And life is too short. I know what I want in life, and God will lead me in His will. If *I* can keep my will surrendered that is," I said, laughing at myself, for that was my greatest struggle.

To my surprise, Dr. McCray laughed warmly. "It is refreshing," he said with a wink.

I smiled. It was the first time a man had said my blunt way of speaking was refreshing. I found myself quite warm and blushing.

"So, as an innocent bystander, as you said, I assume that to mean you have decided to not let me pursue courting you?" he asked, blushing a little himself.

My heart raced for a moment. He was interested in courting me. That was definitely better than just a buggy ride. I sighed, struggling with what my heart ached for, and what my mind told me was best. "But you would be courting Ava as well?" I asked cautiously, unable to look into his eyes for a moment.

"Yes." He didn't even try to sugar coat it.

My heart ached for just a moment. I didn't like the idea of competition; I had never really had to compete at anything. I had always gained the attention of most of the boys in school without ever trying. But apparently, I wasn't enough to convince the handsome doctor he could marry me.

"I like Ava very much; I do not wish to hurt her. She is a gentle spirit, and is quite refined; both are qualities that I do not possess. I can picture you both in the evenings before a fire, Ava at your side, stimulating and intellectual conversation flowing freely. So yes, I am afraid I tend to be quite protective of things I hold dear. I should become an ugly jealous monster if I had to compete for your attentions. I am declining to be pursued," I said honestly with a coy smile. The same smile I knew made most boys melt.

He looked disappointed. "And what do you see you and I doing… if *we* were to be together?" he asked honestly.

My face felt very warm. His question was quite forward; my father would not have liked it one bit. "Well, if it was the same scenario, I would find myself cuddled up beside you in a blanket on the sofa, reading aloud from the latest mystery novel or simply enjoying the quiet crackling of the fire. I do not have the education Ava does, and I am afraid the things I would speak of would soon bore you," I said, fighting not to feel intimidated. I hated feeling intimidated and uneasy.

He looked mesmerized. "And, what things would you speak of?" he whispered.

I was quite uncomfortable now and laughed nervously. "This is all quite silly," I confessed.

He shook his head no and asked that I continue.

"I suppose I would ask of your day, the animals, and the cases that you saw. I would most likely laugh as I told you of my day, the funny little things the children said, if we had them. The adventures of milking the cows and planting the garden, boring things to such a man as yourself." Despite my blushing cheeks I raised my chin high and my eyes met his. "But this is who I am, and I am happy being a farmer's daughter and someday will be happy being a farmer's wife," I said, assuring him I felt no ill towards him and that I was secure in who I was. Only, at the moment, I felt very unsure. This man before me could melt my resolve and intimidate me so quickly.

He stood, solemn, deep in thought, and looked outside the large parlor window.

I turned to look at him and saw a light snow had begun to fall. I jumped to my feet quickly. "Oh, my! Please excuse me, Dr. McCray; I must get home before I cannot see to find my way. I am certain Keane and Georgie do not wish me to be snowed in here," I said breathlessly. It was the truth, along with the truth that I desperately needed to be away from his green eyes and handsome smile.

He helped me put my coat on, and I thanked him. "Well, since you will not allow me to court you, the least I can do is ride with you and see you home," he said tenderly.

"Oh! There is no need. I can take the back fields and get there quickly," I assured him.

He shook his head no. "I will ride with you. I cannot sit snowed in alone, worrying if you made it home, if you're safe. What if you were injured and left lying frozen in the wheat fields? I would much rather leave you warm, at home, dreaming of which farmer you long to marry," he said, teasing me with a wink.

I shook my head at him and smiled. "Although we are not courting, surely we can be friends; I have enjoyed our conversations immensely," I confessed softly.

"I have as well. And, I am honored to call you my friend since you leave me no hope that I might be more. I enjoy being around you, Miss Andley," he said.

I called to Georgie that we were leaving and kissed her cheek goodbye.

Dr. McCray rode alongside of me through the gentle flurries of snow and saw me safely home.

I stood and watched him riding away down our long drive, and my heart ached at just how much I had truly enjoyed my afternoon with him even though I did feel a slight uneasiness around him.

"Best get him out of your head, Valynn Andley; you know it could never work between you," I told myself. *I had to try and forget him.*

CHAPTER TWO

The snow was much too deep to attend church services the next day, and in a way, I was thankful. I dreaded seeing Dr. McCray again, especially since I had been up most the night with only him to occupy my thoughts.

I quickly finished what little chores we did with it being the Sabbath and wished I could go to visit Georgie. I sat down to work on my embroidery and was surprised when I heard sleigh bells shortly after.

My father went to the door, and my heart raced as I heard Dr. McCray's voice. "I wanted to ask your permission to take Valynn on a sleigh ride to Kenrick Farms for a short visit with Keane and Georgiana," he asked my father.

"Of course, Dr. McCray! I am certain Valynn would enjoy the visit. Thank you for coming by for her," Father said, leading him into the parlor where my sisters and I sat sewing.

I was immediately aware of my drab appearance when he walked in looking so handsome, his cheeks red from the cold. I had left my hair down to my waist and wore a simple work dress, knowing we would be home alone, or at least I thought we would be.

I greeted him nervously and couldn't help but return his smile. "Thank you, Dr. McCray! I was just sitting here wishing I could be at Kenrick Farms today. Would you allow me a moment to change?" I asked quickly.

He nodded and joined my father in the kitchen to warm up with a mug of coffee.

I rushed upstairs, my sisters following. They helped me into a heavy muslin dress of dark green and I quickly twisted my long blonde hair into a simple knot at the back of my head, knowing I still looked drab, but not wishing to keep him waiting.

"I thought you said he liked Ava?" Genevieve asked with a smile.

I giggled excitedly and shrugged. Perhaps I had a chance to change his mind after all. I bundled up warmly, kissed my mother's cheek, and promised to come back before dark.

Dr. McCray helped me into the sleigh and covered me with buffalo robes. I couldn't help but smile in excitement as I fastened my winter bonnet.

"I felt I owed you a ride, so I borrowed Dr. Childers' old sleigh. Dr. Anderson purchased a new one, so this one sits at the livery most days," he smiled, as we started down the road.

"Why would you owe me a ride?" I asked, surprised.

He shrugged. "I feel bad that I asked you to take a ride with me and hadn't told you I was also seeing Ava Stein. I should have been honest and upfront with you. And, I must admit, I needed an excuse to see you again," he said with a playful wink.

Oh! There went that crazy fluttering in my stomach again, and I knew this was a bad idea. How could I remain unaffected by him if I spent time in his company? I had to look away.

"Are you sorry I came by?" he asked softly.

I turned to him and shook my head no. "No, I am not sorry," I said, but I knew I was in so much trouble with my heart.

We arrived at Kenrick Farms and were greeted excitedly by Keane and Georgie. We quickly warmed up over mugs of hot cocoa and cinnamon rolls.

"Let's play a card game," Georgiana suggested.

Keane went and found the cards and passed them out as he explained the object of the game.

Georgiana looked at me and smiled. "Now, Dr. McCray, we must forewarn you, Valynn is quite lucky at cards," she said, teasing me. What she really meant to say was that I was very competitive, and he had best watch himself.

I sighed and shook my head. "I have already confessed my evil and competitive nature to Dr. McCray," I said with a wink. I realized just then it must have been flirty of me to wink like that, but he seemed to enjoy the gesture.

After my winning several hands of cards, Keane and Dr. McCray were both getting their feathers ruffled. "How do you do it? Every time, I swear it. She drives me crazy winning every game. I think you cheat, Valynn," Keane said with his face red, but he was laughing.

I feigned shock, and everyone laughed. "You're just a sore loser, Keane Kenrick," I said, dealing the cards once again.

Jori awoke from her nap, and Georgiana handed her to me to hold. I snuggled her closely, drinking in her sweet baby smell, my heart longing for a child of my own. I looked up to see Dr. McCray watching me with a strange look on his face.

"All right, Jori girl, let Aunt Val show you how it is done. Let's take the rest of these sore losers' match sticks," I said, smiling brightly at the good doctor.

He only smiled and shook his head at me. "Remind me not to play with money if Valynn Andley is in the game."

I gasped and then laughed warmly. "Now there is an idea," I teased.

"Do not give her any ideas, Dr. McCray; she would own Kenrick Farms right now if that were the case," Georgie laughed.

"What do you say, Keane, want to play for the farm?" I asked, shocking him and laughing.

Dr. McCray looked surprised and couldn't help but laugh at me. Keane shook his head and turned red; he really hated losing to a girl.

"Was Pastor Crawley announcing the Valentine's dance this morning to those who made it in for services?" I asked, changing the subject.

Dr. McCray suddenly looked interested.

"Yes, though I am not certain how many were able to make it in this weather. But the Larkins will know and Dr. Anderson. I am certain they will help spread the word. I have already told Celia, and she was to tell Eleanor and Matthias and Drew and Millie," Georgie said, following my cue.

I couldn't resist laying my hand on Dr. McCray's arm tenderly. "Do not fear then, good doctor. Ava will be made aware of the dance; you shall not go heartbroken. My sister Celia is married to Ava's oldest brother, John," I said, smiling mischievously.

He smiled in return, patting my hand. "That is a relief, Miss Andley, although I don't mind telling the Steins myself when I join Ava for dinner tonight," he said, throwing my comment right back to me.

Anger nearly overwhelmed me and my face flushed crimson, but I smiled and quickly reminded myself that I had deserved that one. Suddenly, I couldn't help but laugh at my petty jealously, and knowingly, Dr. McCray joined me.

All too soon it was time to leave, and as I kissed my sister goodbye, she whispered in a panic, "Valynn, you must be kind to him if you want his attentions. You preached to me to use my feminine wiles on Keane, and look at you, you're doing the opposite," she warned.

I shook my head and smiled. "He likes Ava, a lot. And we are merely friends. I will not waste my feminine wiles on Dr. McCray," I said, regretting it the moment I said it, for no matter how much I teased and pretended not to like him, I truly did like him, so much.

As Dr. McCray helped me into the sleigh and covered me with the robes, he smiled.

"What are you smiling about?" I asked him, wanting to know what was running through his mind.

He shrugged. "Just thought I might have caught a glimpse of the evil jealous monster you warned me of. But, of course, I was mistaken. You do not wish to court me, so you were not jealous when I said I had plans with Ava this evening," he said, climbing in beside me.

Oh how he infuriated me! Blasted-man! Of course he expected me to deny my jealously, to try to cover it up. I hated these mind games. Isaac had been so simple; I never had to play games with him. "No, you were right. You caught a glimpse of the worst part of me. I told you it was ugly, and I was prone to jealousy," I admitted, shocking him completely.

He shook his head and smiled. "There is not one ugly part of you, Valynn Andley," he assured me, with his green eyes sparkling.

I shook my head no. "I wish that were true, Dr. McCray. I often wish I was more like my sister Celia. I shock her terribly; she is so sweet and pure. She would never degrade herself to be jealous. That is why you and I mustn't see one another too often. You bring out the worst in me, I am afraid," I said, laughing.

To my surprise, Dr. McCray leaned his head back in a deep and oh so thrilling laugh. His eyes met mine, and he shook his head as we pulled up in my parent's drive. "It is a pity, Miss Andley, for I enjoy being with you too much," he said so tenderly my breath caught in my chest.

"Thank you for the afternoon, I truly enjoyed it," I said, standing to leave.

He rushed to help me out just as my foot slipped on the hard packed snow. His strong and capable arms caught me and held me close to his chest so I didn't fall. My heart raced. I wanted to scream at him to let me go. I had enough of his blasted-charming company for one day. He was leaving me to go to Ava. My eyes met his, our faces so close to one another's.

"Goodbye, Dr. McCray," I whispered breathlessly. I was embarrassed he could affect me so.

He simply nodded and walked me safely to the door. "Goodbye, Miss Andley, and thank you for a most enjoyable afternoon," he said, leaving me for Ava.

From my bedroom window upstairs, I watched him drive away, taking my heart with him. Blasted-man!

"Why do you keep looking out the window?" Augusta was truly too nosy for her own good.

I sighed and pretended to be dusting the trim and frowned. "It has snowed another foot at least! I am merely concerned about the weather. At this rate, there will be no dance this weekend," I said. It had snowed for two days, and Dr. McCray had not visited again.

Genevieve giggled. "I think she is looking for Dr. McCray to arrive in his sleigh!" she whispered loud enough so I would be certain to hear her.

Augusta gasped and then giggled. "If Dr. McCray does come for you Valynn, might we go to see Georgie, too?" Augusta asked.

"No!" I said decisively, moving over to dust the piano.

"They cannot kiss if you are with them, Gusta."

I gasped and turned to Genevieve. "We have not kissed! Do not fill her innocent mind with such things," I scolded.

But she sat smiling, pretending to be working on the mending. I could hardly wait to have my own home one day, one to where my younger sisters only visited and didn't keep their cute little noses in my affairs. I closed my eyes and could picture myself sweeping off the porch of the large brick home. I could see Niall McCray, coming out of his office, whisking me into his arms, and asking me what I had cooked for dinner. I smiled, for it was a most pleasant dream.

"Whose wagon is that?" Augusta asked.

I whirled around to the window once more. My sisters joined me as we gawked through the heavily falling snow, trying to determine who was out in such weather.

"It is just Drew Weston and his brother Ben," I said, sighing in great disappointment. Why hadn't Dr. McCray returned to see me? No doubt Ava had seen him. The thought made me truly angry…. and jealous.

"Valynn," my mother called to me.

I sighed and went into the kitchen.

"The Weston boys are here; go and offer them a cup of coffee and a slice of pie to warm up with," she said, smiling.

I frowned but did as she asked. They would no doubt be cold. What were they doing out in this weather anyhow?

I didn't bother changing my shoes or putting on my coat. I grabbed a thin shawl and stepped out the kitchen door, opening my mouth to call for Drew, but snow filled it quickly. I tried once more and groaned as I realized I would have to walk out to them.

My father was with them now, and it appeared they had brought over a load of firewood. "Father," I called out. All three men turned to look at me just as I stepped down into the deep drift, not realizing how much it had truly snowed. I sank to my thighs and fell forward, face first into the snow.

"Val!" my father called out.

Strong arms lifted me up as I laughed, wiping the snow from my face. Gentle brown eyes met mine with a tender smile as Ben Weston lifted me into his arms.

"Oh!" I said, not expecting him to do such a thing. But I supposed I *had* been stuck.

"Are you all right, Valynn?" he asked, carrying me toward the back door.

I nodded and smiled. "Just clumsy as always," I blushed.

My father walked behind us, smiling, and I groaned, knowing what he was thinking. Ben was a farmer, was settled, and was carrying me in his arms. No doubt my father was planning our wedding and how many loads of wood he would get out of the deal.

Ben sat me on the back steps and helped me to open the kitchen door. I was shivering now as my underskirts were soaked.

"Valynn, what on earth happened?" Mother rushed to me with a small towel and began to brush the snow from my long hair and face.

I laughed warmly.

"She sank into a drift, Mrs. Andley." Ben's smile told me he found the entire situation quite funny. He would! He was the same pain in the backside he used to be, throwing frogs on me, terrifying me. Not at all the charming mature man Niall McCray was.

"Go on up and get dry. Ben, would you and Drew like a slice of pie and a cup of coffee?"

My eyes met Ben's, and he grinned. "I would love a piece, Mrs. Andley."

I marched upstairs wondering how someone like Ben could be so handsome and yet so ornery. I took my time changing my clothes and drying my hair with a towel. It was most likely rude of me, but I was so disappointed in Dr. McCray. He had truly acted as if he liked me and had enjoyed our day at Kenrick Farms. He had a sleigh, for heaven's sakes. Ben and Drew had made it out in a wagon. There was no excuse for his not coming, except for one- Ava Stein.

By the time I returned to the kitchen, Drew and Ben had left and were unloading the wood for my father.

"My, that Ben Weston has grown into a handsome young man." My mother's blushing cheeks and bright eyes caused me to groan. *Here we went.*

"Yes, Margaret, that he has," my father agreed, too quickly. "And so strong he is. Why he lifted our Val up so easily, carried her like it was nothing."

I rolled my eyes as I helped myself to a piece of pie.

"Millie and Eleanor said his house is quite nice. Seems he would be looking to marry soon," my mother smiled over her coffee cup.

I sat down and licked the fork. My mother made the best pies, well, next to Georgie's anyway.

"Has Ben been seeing anyone, Valynn?" she asked sweetly.

"How am I supposed to know?" I asked.

She sighed at my lack of interest and frowned.

"He was watching our Val; he got to her when she fell before I could hardly move one foot," father said, smiling.

I laughed; they were trying very hard to get me to like Ben Weston. "You *are* getting older, Father dear," I said, patting his hand tenderly.

He smiled, for he knew I was on to their shenanigans.

"Ben Weston is a pain in the backside, mark my words!" I said, stuffing a bite of flaky goodness into my mouth.

"Valynn!" my mother said, appalled.

My father shook his head. He had given up on me long ago.

"We do not discuss backsides at the table or anywhere else for that matter!" she scolded.

I met my father's smile and shook my head.

"It looks like someone as strong and as handsome as Ben Weston would surely have a desire to marry."

I sighed; she wasn't going to let it go. "He probably *does* have the desire, but no one will have him. Need I remind you of his frog fascination? He terrifies girls!" I declared.

Father burst into laughter and Mother jumped to her feet, giving up on convincing me that Ben Weston was a good catch. He was, perhaps, if you loved frogs, but I didn't. I shuddered at the thought.

That evening I was terribly restless. What would a single man be doing on a snowy night alone? It couldn't be better than an evening of card games at Kenrick farms, along with Georgie's cooking, I was certain of that.

"Come and play with us, Val!" Augusta called from the dining room table.

I sighed and shook my head. I wasn't in the mood to play games this night.

"Come on, Valynn. You have been moping all day. He isn't going to come this late, you know!" Genevieve taunted.

I sighed and decided to shut them up. I joined my family at the table and took the die to start a new game. A knock sounded at the back door, and I jumped to my feet, racing to the door. My heart nearly stopped, for there before me was Niall McCray, dusted from head to toe with snow.

"Come in, Dr. McCray!" I said, much too eagerly.

"Good evening, Miss Andley. I pray I am not calling too late," he said as his eyes searched mine.

I could hardly breathe. "No, come on in," I said, shaking my head. How could he disorient me so quickly?

I took his coat as Mother rushed to fix him a cup of tea. Genevieve brought him the last slice of the pie as my Father settled him at the table with us.

"I am sorry to come by so late, but I was just out at the Weston farm, and they mentioned bringing a load of firewood over here," Dr. McCray said, looking at me with a devious grin.

I gasped. Had Ben told him of my fall in the snow? He smiled, and I suddenly knew Ben had. Blasted-men! My cheeks warmed as I looked at my mother. She merely smiled.

"Yes, the Weston boys are good to keep me stocked during the winter months," my father said.

Dr. McCray nodded but didn't take his eyes off of me. Would he ask me to the dance this night? I prayed he would, surely he would. "Could I borrow a few sticks? I will pay you, of course."

I frowned. He drove all the way out here, this late, in the snow, for a couple of sticks of wood that he could have gotten from Drew himself. I suddenly smiled. *He missed me*!

"Why, of course, Dr. McCray. You are welcome to as much as you need. No need to pay us. Valynn, walk Dr. McCray out to the barn," my father said.

I felt my cheeks warm even more. I stood and tried to compose myself, but it truly was impossible. I bundled up warmly and Dr. McCray held my elbow as he helped me toward the barn. My father should have been doing this, but I smiled as I realized he knew I liked Niall McCray. He was giving us a few moments alone, no doubt so Niall would ask me to the dance.

"It is a beautiful night," I said softly.

He nodded as our eyes met. I looked over to see he had come in the sleigh. I smiled again. Wood indeed! My heart raced with excitement.

Niall opened the barn door, and I smiled as the warmth and the smell of hay greeted us. Niall smiled, and for the first time, he seemed a bit nervous.

"Well, how many sticks of wood do you need, Dr. McCray?" I asked. No more than a small armful would fit in that little sleigh.

"Three," he said.

I smiled. "Just three?" Why three? The man was ridiculous.

He nodded and loaded his arms.

I frowned. He couldn't kiss me with his arms full of wood.

"This should do me for tonight," he said.

"What was wrong at the Weston farm? Their horse didn't hurt its leg in this snow, did it?" I asked, stalling him. He couldn't have possibly driven over here for three sticks of wood!

Niall shook his head no. "I was at the Steins for dinner and heard they had come by here with wood," he said.

I felt my cheeks warm. He had eaten with Ava, and he had wished me to know it. My temper was getting the best of me. We were completely out of the way, especially for three sticks of wood.

"What did Ben Weston have to say?" he asked.

I frowned again. "He said hello," I said blandly. I hated these stupid games.

"Oh, after he carried to the door, or before?" he asked.

I burst into laughter. "I knew it!" I said.

Niall frowned and walked toward the door.

"You missed me, and you were jealous to hear Ben had stopped by!" I accused.

Niall turned around. "I needed wood, Miss Andley, do not flatter yourself."

Oh, how I wanted to slap his handsome face! "Yes, and there is no wood to be had at the Stein farm, is there? Nor, at the Weston farm!" I said, still laughing.

Niall stared at me, his cheeks flamed red. "Goodnight, Miss Andley."

"I think you just got a taste of your own medicine, Dr. McCray!" I declared.

He paused at the barn door but did not turn to look at me.

"It really isn't pleasant, is it?" I asked. I was enjoying his jealously, too much really.

"No, not at all, Miss Andley. Goodnight!"

I listened as his sleigh left our yard and then picked up the lantern to walk back to the house. It suddenly dawned on me; he hadn't asked me to the dance. I sighed in disappointment, and yet I could not stop smiling.

Niall McCray might like Ava, but he hadn't driven miles out of his way for three sticks of wood just to see her. *But he had for me!*

I was upstairs cleaning the next afternoon, restless, and hoping every second to hear the familiar sleigh bells pulling up into our drive. My hair was tied up in a kerchief, and I was terribly dusty. Spring was nearly two months away, and the house desperately needed a good scrubbing and airing. But with all this snow, it seemed as if winter would last an eternity. I was beginning to hate snow. I hadn't been to Kenrick Farms in days.

"Valynn, Mother says to come down, you have a visitor."

I smiled and rushed to the mirror, tearing off my kerchief and dusting off my dress, and then pinching my cheeks.

Augusta stood smiling as she watched me.

"I didn't hear the sleigh," I said, rushing toward the back stairs.

"He didn't come in a sleigh," she said.

I didn't wait to ask her more. My heart raced and matched my feet as I rushed downstairs, and breathlessly ran straight into Ben Weston.

He smiled and steadied me on my feet.

My eyes searched the room frantically.

"Valynn, Ben has stopped by to see you," mother said, silently urging me to be friendly with her piercing blue eyes.

I forced my smile and looked to Augusta. She smiled brightly, *the little stinker*. She knew I had thought it was Dr. McCray, and yet she said nothing.

"Ben, what a pleasant surprise!" I said, trying to smile and not show my disappointment that he had not been Dr. McCray.

"Hello, Valynn! It is good to see you again," he smiled.

He looked handsome this day in a dark grey flannel coat with black trim. But he was still Ben, still ornery; still Frog Ben. I doubted I could ever get past the fact.

"What brings you out in this weather?" I asked, shocked that he was here, in a snowstorm, in my kitchen.

"I brought another load of firewood out to your father. I was hoping perhaps I could speak with you," he said.

I held my breath. "Of course, Ben. Would you like to go into the parlor?" I asked.

"Valynn, go and help Ben unload the wood. Then you may talk in the parlor over coffee," mother urged.

I gave her my best annoyed look. "Yes, Mother." I walked to where the coats hung near the back door.

Ben was kind and helped me into my coat. "You do not need to help me with the wood, Valynn. Some of the pieces are quite heavy."

I smiled as I looked at his sincere face. He was rather sweet. "I do not mind, Ben."

Once we were outside, Ben took my arm and helped me down the back steps and through the snow. "It is much too heavy work for a lady," he said.

I laughed warmly. "I am used to hard work, Ben. I am a farmer's daughter!"

He smiled tenderly. "You shouldn't have to work so hard."

I could see he was sincere, and somehow it warmed my heart toward him, just a little. We reached the wagon and to my surprise, Ben lifted me and set me on the seat. "Ben Weston! I am quite able to unload wood," I insisted.

His smile was rather handsome. "I know. I will unload, you can keep those little feet dry, and we can talk," he said nervously.

I smiled. Ben Weston was shy! I watched as his muscles flexed beneath his heavy coat as he reached and lifted large chunks of wood. Ben was a big man, tall, strong, *very strong*. He was actually well made and handsome. I looked away as my cheeks burned. "What was it you were wanting to talk to me about?" I asked.

Ben nodded. "Right," he said, pausing in his work.

My heart went out to him, for he was clearly struggling although I had no idea why.

"I came by yesterday, to talk to you."

I raised an eyebrow in surprise. I thought he had come to unload wood. "Why didn't you then?" I asked softly.

He blushed and nodded, and then looked up at me with a tender smile. "I tried," he admitted.

His words touched me somehow and I smiled but wondered why Ben hadn't succeeded. "Well, I am listening now," I said, trying to ease him.

He nodded and bit his bottom lip. It was terribly cute. "Would you consider going to the Valentine's Dance with me, Valynn?" he sighed heavily and grabbed the wagon as if it had taken all his strength to ask me such a thing.

My heart sank, for I was truly hoping to go with Dr. McCray. But he had yet to ask me. Ben was here first, and looking at his anxious face now, I could not turn him down. Even I was not that cruel. I forced a smiled and nodded.

"I would like that, Ben, thank you," I said, wishing I felt something for this man before me. He had a nice farm, and I had heard he had built his own farmhouse last year soon after his brother Drew and Millie's home had been blown away in a storm. He was what I should want for my future. Why couldn't I?

"Great! That is great news, Valynn," he said, beginning to unload the wood once more.

"Oh, Ben, I will most likely be at Kenrick Farms helping Georgie with the preparations; would it be all right for you to meet me there?" I asked.

He smiled and nodded. "You know, Dr. McCray came by last night," he said.

I felt myself sit up a little straighter. "For wood?" I asked.

Ben frowned, confused, and shook his head no. "Someone had told him we had a sick horse. He never said who. He asked a lot of strange questions of why we had come over here earlier in the day."

I couldn't believe the nerve of that no-good-horse-doctoring-Romeo! He told me he had gone for wood, but Drew and Ben always had extra wood to sell. There would have been no need to come to Andley Farms. He was jealous, and this proved it. "What did you tell him?" I asked, not truly thinking, but knowing Ben stood waiting for a reaction from me.

He sighed. "I told him the truth, that we came to deliver wood."

I nodded, still deep in thought of how the doctor must care for me.

"Are you seeing Dr. McCray, Valynn?" he asked softly, perhaps hesitantly.

I shook my head no, but my heart ached with the truth, for I wished I was seeing him. "He is courting Ava Stein," I said, feeling the evil jealous monster rising up within me once again. I hated feeling this way.

Ben nodded and began to work once more. "He said as much."

I stiffened. "Did he say anything else?" I asked.

Ben shook his head. "It was just his odd questioning. It made me think that perhaps you two had an understanding, and he didn't want me stepping in."

I smiled, knowing very well what Niall McCray was up to. I shook my head no. We had no understanding, *not yet*.

Ben smiled. "Good, it is good to hear." He smiled such a tender smile and somehow it made my heart flutter just a little. "It is cold out here, Valynn. Let me walk you back inside." He took my elbow and helped me back into the kitchen. He bid us all a goodnight and rushed to unload the wood before dark.

My father stood watching from the kitchen window and smiled. "I wonder why Ben would bring me another wagon load of wood when he just brought one yesterday."

I blushed and smiled. "He asked me to go to the dance Saturday evening," I said, kissing my father's cheek.

My mother smiled, pleased.

"Well, if he brings a load each time he comes over, I shouldn't need wood until Augusta weds."

I slapped my father's arm playfully. "It is just a dance, and he is *just Ben*. We are friends, sort of," I said. I had never considered Ben a friend, not after the frogs those years ago.

I closed my eyes, remembering that day so long ago at the creek where a large group of us had been swimming. Ben had found a mess of tree frogs and threw them on me, their sticky feet plastering themselves to my skin. I had screamed as if I was being eaten alive. The embarrassment he caused me, and fear of frogs, still lived within me to this day.

I shuddered as I walked out of the kitchen. It would be wrong not to forgive him, but I was thankful it was cold, for there was no way he could find frogs in this weather. "He *will not* be coming over all the time!" I called out to my parents.

I stopped on the stairwell and looked out the window into the backyard. The sun was setting, and if he didn't hurry, he would still be unloading the wood in the darkness. I sighed heavily and shook my head. Why *had* Ben brought another load of wood out if my father hadn't asked him to?

I groaned and rushed back down the stairs, grabbing my coat and heading toward Ben and the wagon.

"Valynn, what are you doing back out here?" he asked, rushing to help me through the drifts.

I sighed; I truly didn't know what I was doing. "Let me take all the smaller pieces, and together, we can have this done by dark."

Ben smiled, pleased, and nodded.

We were nearly done, with only a few bigger pieces of wood left to unload, when I rolled a small handful of snow in my hand. "Ben!" I called.

He turned smiling, and I hit my target, right in the eye. I gasped and then burst into laughter as Ben wiped the snowball from his eye.

"What did you put in that thing? A rock?" he accused.

I couldn't stop laughing. "Vengeance is mine!" I said, raising my arms like a victor.

Ben laughed and yanked me from the wagon, tossing me over his shoulder like a sack of grain.

I squealed for him to put me down, but he laughed all the way to the kitchen door. He sat me on my feet, very close to his chest. His warm brown eyes smiled at me with such sincerity, I had to smile in return.

"Thank you, Valynn."

I raised an eyebrow. "For what, giving you a black eye?" I reached out to touch his now red and puffy eye. "I am sorry, Ben. I suppose I threw it harder than I thought!"

He smiled and shook his head. "It was worth it," he said softly.

I suddenly wondered why there was no air out here this cold night.

"You will still go to the dance with me, even if I have a black eye, won't you, Valynn?"

I laughed and nodded. "I have to… it is my fault!"

He smiled and lifted my hand to his lips. I wasn't prepared for that. I didn't want Ben to think I liked him in that way. I didn't want to hurt him, but I was afraid I had lost my heart to an arrogant two-timing veterinarian.

"Goodnight, Valynn. Sweet dreams."

I nodded, trying to calm the flutters in my stomach. "Goodnight, Ben."

But it was a restless night for me. Not only was I worried over Niall McCray asking me to the dance, and my having to refuse him, I now had to worry about hurting Frog Ben's feelings. *Blasted-men!*

CHAPTER THREE

The snow finally melted, and by the end of the week, I had plans to join Georgie, Eleanor, Celia and Millie at Kenrick Farms to resolve the final preparations for the Valentine's dance the next evening.

I was just leading my mare into the barn to Henry when I heard a familiar voice call for me. "Miss Andley! How nice to see you today," Dr. McCray said from behind me.

I turned and couldn't help but smile. I had missed seeing him. My thoughts had continually been of him. "Good morning, Dr. McCray. It is nice to see you as well," I said, nervous and a bit uneasy now. But why? I didn't understand these feelings he seemed to provoke in me. I didn't know that I liked this uneasiness, but I was certain I liked him, very much. I had practiced smiling and nodding as he asked me to dance, over and over in front of the mirror, in my mind of course.

"Have you come to help with the dance preparations?" he asked.

I suddenly noticed he was helping Keane to hang lanterns in the rafters as lighting for the dance. "Yes, Georgie asked me to come," I said, smiling. Perhaps he would be around all day, and that thought made me happy. Would he ask me to the dance? My heart ached at the thought of being in his arms waltzing.

"Of course," he said, smiling and blushing.

I bit my lip at seeing his nervousness. I had missed him so. "Did your three sticks of wood keep you warm, Dr. McCray?" I asked with a mischievous grin.

He laughed and blushed even deeper, nodding. "You will not let me forget this, will you?" he asked.

I smiled and shook my head no. Didn't he see that I liked him? We needn't play these silly games with one another.

"I would have liked for *you* to have kept me warm, Miss Andley."

I felt my breath leave my body and my cheeks burn crimson. He was really too bold. He chuckled at my blush, and I held my breath.

"Perhaps that is Ava's job," I said bitterly. What kind of girl did he think I was? I was bold in speech, but that was as far as it went.

But Niall McCray merely watched me, amused, delighting in my naïve ways. I looked away.

"I do need to confess something to you, Miss Andley; I have asked Ava to the dance," he said awkwardly now.

I felt as if the wind had been knocked out of me. But I nodded and smiled. "That is wonderful! I am certain you will both have a good time. I am going with Ben Weston, or rather, he is my escort but meeting me here," I stammered, wanting him to know I already had a date.

"Oh! Ben Weston, yes, delivering more than wood, I suppose," he said, appearing in deep thought. "He is a good man," he admitted.

I forced my smile. "Yes he is," I agreed, perhaps a little too excitedly. I had enough of this. "Well, I will let you get back to work, Dr. McCray. I hear giggling indoors and must join in," I said, smiling brightly although I did not feel happy inside at all. How dare he ask Ava over me? And how dare he say such a bold thing to me as my keeping him warm?

"Of course, I will see you tomorrow night then," he said.

I nodded and left quickly for the house. I needed my friend's laughter to help me forget the ache inside my heart. How stupid I was to be infatuated with a man too old for me and bold enough to court more than one girl at a time. Blasted-man!

As I helped put icing on the heart shaped sugar cookies in Georgie's kitchen, I smiled and enjoyed the light conversation between friends. My sister Celia and our friends Eleanor and Millie had all given birth within six weeks of each other. Celia had been first birthing my nephew Johnny. Eleanor was next with her daughter Sadie and then Millie with her son Will. They would all be turning one year in the soon coming spring. Even my sister Georgie now had three-month old Jori, and I found myself feeling a little left out being the only unwed one present.

"Dr. McCray is out in the barn, Val," I heard Georgiana say.

I nodded and continued my task at hand. "I spoke with him," I said softly.

"Why would Val want to know that Dr. McCray was here?" I heard Eleanor ask, surprised.

I blushed profusely.

"Oh, truly?" Eleanor asked, looking at me and realizing I must have feelings for the veterinarian.

I shook my head no. "No, you are jumping to conclusions. We are friends, well, not even friends really. He is taking Ava to the dance, and Ben Weston is escorting me," I said, putting their wandering minds to ease.

Eleanor sighed. "Oh Val, I am so sorry about Isaac. Mother and Father Stein have been very angry with his decisions. I heard Father Stein yelling at Isaac the day he left for the gold mines, telling him he was losing a good girl," Eleanor said softly. "I did so want you for my sister-in-law," she admitted.

I smiled and thanked her. "I am not heartbroken, Ellie. I feel relieved that he left in many ways. I think it was meant to be this way," I admitted.

"Well, I for one think Isaac will wake up and realize his mistake and come running back to you, Valynn. He has adored you for years," my sister Celia said. She was married to Isaac's older brother John. She shook her head as if men puzzled her.

"I told him I would not wait, and I am not waiting," I assured her firmly. I couldn't even think of Isaac now that I had seen Dr. McCray's green eyes so close to mine.

"Well, I for one am happy to hear you're going to the dance with Ben. I would love to have you as a sister-in-law," Millie said, smiling warmly.

I thanked her but quickly assured her I only sought Ben's friendship.

"So, if you have feelings for Dr. McCray, does he know it?" Eleanor asked with concern. "I am just asking because of Ava; she is smitten with him. They spend quite a lot of time together. She expects a proposal any day now even though Father Stein would rather her marry a man back East," Eleanor said cautiously.

I sighed. I had to admit that this news upset me just a little. "I have mixed feelings for him. I had contemplated his attentions until I saw him with Ava. He had asked to take me on a buggy ride. I hadn't known he was also seeing Ava until recently. He doesn't see anything wrong with dating around. I did accept a sleigh ride to Kenrick Farms, but that is all. He mentioned courting, but I wouldn't consent. I told him I wouldn't hurt Ava," I said, still unable to deny my attraction to the infuriating man.

"Good for you, Valynn! A man who dates so many women at one time can only mean trouble," Millie assured me.

I nodded, wishing I could make my heart believe that very thing. Just how much time was he spending with Ava?

To my horror, Dr. McCray stayed all afternoon working with Keane and Henry. I was spending the night at Kenrick Farms to help Georgie, so that night at supper when Keane invited Dr. McCray to stay, Dr. McCray graciously accepted with a mischievous grin.

I tried my best to act disinterested in him; the man was too confident in himself, I was certain.

The conversation flowed freely, and I soon found myself unable to stay mad and uninterested in Dr. McCray. He was much too charming. Keane brought out the cards, and we played a few hands, with me winning each time. I hadn't laughed so hard in a very long time and found myself blushing as I caught Dr. McCray watching me intensely.

Georgie excused herself to nurse Jori in the bedroom, and Keane went back out to the barn to do his evening chores. I was left alone at the table with Dr. McCray.

"So, it is Ben now, is it?" he asked, catching me off guard.

I raised my chin higher and smiled. *He was jealous.* "It is for tomorrow evening, at least," I smiled brightly.

He nodded. "Have you heard from Isaac since he left?" he asked me.

I shook my head no. Why did everyone assume I was heartbroken over Isaac? "I do not expect to hear from him. He was quite devastated that I wouldn't wait for him," I said, playing with the cards in my hand.

"So what does Ben have that Isaac does not?" he asked me.

I frowned. "Why are you so interested in my affairs, Dr. McCray?" I asked, annoyed.

He shrugged and smiled, making my stomach quiver, and I wanted to slap him. "I find you fascinating, Miss Andley," he admitted.

I had to laugh. "Well, I am far from fascinating, Dr. McCray, and you shouldn't say such things to me. What about Ava?" I asked, raising my eyebrow to him in question.

He sighed. "I have promised her nothing. She knows I asked you for a buggy ride and that you turned me down flat," he said, chuckling.

"I did take a sleigh ride with you," I offered with a smile.

He nodded. "And I truly enjoyed our time together," he said, making me blush.

I stiffened. I didn't like these games he played, not at all. "I think Ava expects more," I said softly.

He gave me a weak smile. "I cannot offer her more at this time," he confessed.

I wanted to ask him why, but I was afraid to know. Perhaps there were several other women involved in his playing around the field, and it would only prove to break my heart even more.

"So, back to my question. What does Ben Weston have that Isaac doesn't?" he asked again.

I sighed and thought deeply about it. "I haven't really compared them. This is the first time Ben has asked me to go with him anywhere. Ben does have his own house and a nice farm. Although he is not a wealthy Stein, he owns his land. He seems ready to settle down, and of course, we know Isaac wasn't. They are both good Christian men. They would both make someone a fine husband. Well, if Isaac were to settle down," I said with a chuckle.

"How long have you known Ben?" Dr. McCray asked, observing me closely as if I was one of his four-legged patients.

"Most of my life, I suppose. We grew up together, went to school together. He is a few years older than I," I said, wondering when his questioning would stop and why I felt compelled to answer them.

"And does Ben make you blush when he looks into your eyes?" he asked softly.

I gasped. He had gone too far once again. "I am afraid that is none of your business, Dr. McCray. Would you like coffee?" I asked, standing.

He quickly grabbed my hand in his, and I felt my cheeks blush. I wanted to curse. He chuckled, and I knew what he was doing. He was forcing me to prove that I was attracted to him. Blasted-man!

"Stop that!" I said, chastising him and pouring us both a cup of coffee.

"Why won't you let me come courting you, Miss Andley? I know you're attracted to me," Dr. McCray asked me with a confident grin.

I felt my cheeks growing warm. Was there no end to his aggravating manners? I sighed and shook my head. Why indeed? I had to breathe in deeply and remind myself why I was struggling to avoid this handsome man before me. "Because… I deserve to be the only one. I will not share the man I court with another woman. I deserve better than that. If you truly liked me, you wouldn't pursue anyone else," I said, looking into his green eyes but feeling uneasy and intimidated once again. *I didn't like feeling this way.*

"But I truly like you, Miss Andley, very much," he confessed.

I raised my chin higher. My heart raced to hear his words, and yet I didn't know if he even truly knew his own feelings. "But not enough! I know you spend a lot of time with Ava. If you like Ava so much, then why are you doing this to me?" I asked him bluntly. "Why put me through this?" I asked, getting irritated.

"I want to make the right decision. I enjoy my time with Ava, but then I see you, and I cannot forget you. There is something between us. You cannot deny it," he admitted.

Keane came back in just in time to save me from answering the aggravating man. Dr. McCray stood and bid us both a goodnight. I allowed Keane to walk him to the door, and I went upstairs to the room where I stayed when I came to Kenrick Farms.

What an infuriating man he was. He was intent on breaking my heart, and I was doing a good job of letting him. Blasted-man! I lay awake most of the night praying for wisdom and praying for discernment. I wanted nothing more than to be Mrs. Dr. McCray, and yet there was a strange uneasiness I found I could hardly ignore. Did a Godly gentleman court two women at once? Did they say bold things like *keeping each other warm*? My cheeks blushed crimson just thinking of it. I was afraid I knew the answer, and yet my heart ached with want to excuse his behavior. *I had never been so confused.*

The next morning I awoke, determined I was going to put Dr. McCray out of my mind. I found him attractive, there was no doubt. The fact that he was so confident in knowing I found him attractive infuriated me. Something seemed amiss with him. He was flirting with me while Ava assumed they were courting. And although I did believe he was interested in me, I could not condone his actions, nor could I explain the uneasiness I felt in his presence.

So I decided, tonight I would enjoy the dance, be friendly to Ben, and truly have a good time. I would not waste a good dance on the likes of Niall McCray!

I jumped in and helped Georgie with breakfast and cuddled with my sweet niece as Georgie took a bath and washed her hair. We took turns rolling each other's hair in rag curlers and ironed our dresses. I was in love with my new dress. It was so pretty in the pale pink plaid. The black velvet trimmings made it look expensive, and I could hardly wait to wear it.

When Jori went down for a nap, Mormor came to watch over her as Georgie and I went out and decorated the barn. We draped red tissue streamers and hung large paper hearts on the barn walls. We covered tables with red gingham tablecloths and added candles.

"I am sorry Dr. McCray did not ask you to the dance, Val. But Ben is a good man. I think if you gave him a chance, you might find you could like him. Perhaps there is something between Dr. McCray and Ava after all, just as Eleanor said," Georgie said tenderly.

I hated how jealous I suddenly felt. I did not like this feeling of competition, and it did not make me behave well. So much for me determining not to think of him this day, blasted-man! I was in the loft hanging a large red heart from a beam. What was lacking in me that I wasn't enough for him? Isaac had never seemed to find me lacking in anything. If he had, he had been too afraid to say so. Was Ava prettier than I was? Surely he was mature enough not to like a girl solely for her looks. I frowned, perhaps he wasn't. Was I too rough, being a farmer's daughter? Perhaps it was the elegance Ava exuded or her inability to get dirty. I suddenly laughed.

"Well, perhaps the handsome doctor doesn't like farm girls; perhaps he likes snooty, refined women who don't know the back end of a horse from the front?" I said spitefully. I felt nearly evil thinking of Ava and Dr. McCray together, and I knew it was not Christian-like, but I couldn't seem to help myself. I shook my head full of rag curlers dramatically and cleared my throat, getting Georgie's attention.

"What am I to do, dear handsome Doctor? I have never stepped a satin slipper in a barn before! Oh my! You want me to milk this cow? From which end does the milk come? Oh my! Why I couldn't possibly touch such a thing. I might soil my French gown and dirty my daintily gloved hands," I said, waltzing down the steps of the loft theatrically, acting like Ava Stein. "Please do go bathe, handsome Doctor; you smell like animals. Why do you always smell like animals?" I asked in the best snooty voice I could muster.

Georgie was nearly rolling in laughter as I continued my theatrics. It was mean and I knew I was going to have to repent. And to my dismay, I didn't feel any better.

"Did you just speak of a brood mare at my dinner table, dear Doctor? I daresay I am not used to such talk. It is sending me into vapors; I am too refined and elegant to speak of filthy farm animals. Do hush now and kiss me," I said, bursting into giggles until a very masculine throat cleared. I whirled around on the last step, and to my horror, it was Dr. McCray!

Georgie stopped laughing, and my cheeks burned crimson, knowing he had to have heard a little of my evil theatrics. Georgie quickly excused herself and all but ran out of the barn. I knew I had been left to face my sins alone.

But to my surprise, Dr. McCray did not look angry, but perhaps amused.

I raised my chin a little higher than I should have and stepped off the stairs, not really watching my feet. To add to my discomfort, I tripped and fell to my knees in the hay. Warm masculine laughter rang out through the barn as strong hands came under my arms lifting me up to my feet. *I was beyond mortified.* I slowly lifted my eyes to his, hating that he had seen such an ugly and spiteful side of me. "Thank you," I said, trying to back away, but his arms held me firmly.

"Perhaps I should make certain you are all right first. I am a doctor of sorts, even if it is to filthy farm animals," he said softly.

I shook my head in embarrassment, and to my horror, saw rag curlers flying from both sides of my shoulders. I groaned and covered my face. There was no end to my humiliation.

He laughed heartily and took one of my curlers in his fingers. "This is a new look," he said, amused.

"I am fine now. Thank you," I said, bolting from him only to find him smiling at me and enjoying my agony.

He chuckled, and I shook my head again. "Please forgive me, Dr. McCray. You have now seen me at my very worst, and now you know, the evil jealous monster in me does indeed exist. Please know I shall leave you now and go and repent," I said, trying to leave the barn, but he caught my hand in his, laughing.

"Even at your worst, you are the most beautiful sight I have beheld," he said softly.

I looked at him surprised; he thought I was beautiful, even in rag curlers. He was leaning in towards me, and I felt quite uneasy. "Even cruelly making fun of your girl? I do not think so, and I am completely ashamed. I told you that you brought out the worst in me," I said, completely embarrassed.

"Valynn," he whispered.

I had to look away; for some reason I felt he was very close to kissing me. I longed for his kiss. Yet I was frightened he might do so and deepen this strange uneasiness and attraction I held for him. Something didn't feel right. Why couldn't this feel right?

He looked disappointed that I wouldn't let him close. "Please do not say I bring out the worst in you. I do not wish to hear that. And about Ava, that was truly evil of you, but you know her too well, I fear," he said as if I had opened his eyes to her downfalls.

"No, she is a good woman. I do like her. I let my jealousy take control and I had no right. I am sorry," I said, owning my sins.

Dr. McCray's mouth twisted in a smile. "I do wish *I* was escorting *you* tonight," he said tenderly.

I looked surprised. "You could have asked me," I said bluntly.

He nodded. "Things aren't as simple as they seem, Valynn," he said, using my first name although I had not given him leave to, but I could not deny him. I liked how he said my name; there was a certain tenderness behind it.

"Well, I suppose the more women you court, the less simple life becomes," I teased but truly meant it.

He smiled and his cheeks colored a little. "True. I am certain my circumstances are of my own making," he said, sighing. "If Ben will agree, will you save me a waltz tonight?" he asked tenderly.

My mind raced. How could I keep from falling for this man if I continued to let him get close to me? The uneasiness overwhelmed me suddenly, and I felt I had to get away from him. "Perhaps," I said, trying to leave.

He once again stopped me. "You promise not to embarrass me by denying me in front of everyone? I fear they all know you already denied me a buggy ride," he said, looking hurt and vulnerable.

I had to get out of there. "Well, you know it is my life's mission to embarrass you, Dr. McCray," I teased. "You have seen how evil I truly am; do not expect me to behave properly," I said, laughing and breaking free from him.

"Valynn, I suggest you leave the curlers in. Ben will like them," he teased.

I gasped in feign shock. "I am glad it is you who saw me looking like this, for if Ben had seen me, no doubt I would be without an escort tonight," I said, making my way towards the door.

"I doubt that. Ben knows a good thing when he sees it. He is a wise man; he acts upon his desires, a wise man indeed," he said, throwing me off again.

It almost sounded as if he were truly jealous of Ben. I could only nod, for that was the difference between Niall McCray and Ben Weston. Ben was going after what he wanted which was to escort me to the dance. Dr. McCray had said he wished it were he escorting me, but he had not cared enough to ask, nor to give up courting Ava.

I left the barn before he could say anything else. I had decided to put Dr. McCray out of my mind, and I had failed terribly.

"So, what did Dr. McCray say about your little theatrics in the barn?" Georgie asked as she helped me to style my long hair.

I sighed, blushed, and then shook my head, smiling. "I have repented of my ways, Georgie. He was not angry, to my surprise. He even seemed a bit amused. He enjoys that I am jealous of Ava. I do not understand him. He knows I am attracted to him, and it irritates me to no end. He speaks of wanting to court me, wishing he was taking me to the dance but will not give up Ava. He flirts with me in a most improper way. I cannot help but feel thrilled, uneasy, and disappointed all at the same time. I feel intimidated when I am with him and I do not think I should," I admitted, deep in thought.

Georgie shook her head. "He seems to be playing with your affections, Valynn. I cannot admire that in a man. I do not know what to think of him, except, that if he truly wished to court you, he would give up Ava," she said to me tenderly.

I nodded. "I have to agree although it stings me to say so. When I am near him, I feel something isn't quite right. There is attraction for certain, an excitement I have never known, but an underlying uneasiness that I cannot explain. I think he nearly kissed me in the barn. And it is evil of me, but I had wanted him to... until the uneasiness returned. I had to get away from him. I can't explain why, but I just knew I had to," I said, sighing.

Georgie giggled. "Resist the devil and he will flee from you. James 4:7," she said, referring to Dr. McCray as a devil.

Perhaps that was why I was feeling uneasy, perhaps Mormor was right. What if Dr. McCray did not have good intentions towards me? He wasn't asking my father to court me, and he was calling me by my first name without permission. He had made the embarrassing comment about me keeping him warm. And now, I was certain that he nearly kissed me in the barn. I hated to admit it, but he was a devil indeed. How could I have not seen the signs before? Was I that naïve?

I sighed as I realized I simply hadn't wanted to see his flaws. I had tried to excuse his behavior over and over because of the strong attraction I held for him. But I had to ask myself, was he was honorable, trustworthy, and loyal? Was he a good man, like my father? My heart ached for I knew he wasn't. I could no longer make excuses for his behavior. What a mess I had gotten myself into. I had never known a man like Niall McCray, and now, I wished I had never met the devil!

I looked in the mirror at my reflection and was pleased with my new dress, the way I had styled my long blonde curls loosely behind my head in a soft pink ribbon. I had taken extra care in dressing tonight, wishing Dr. McCray would be beside himself watching me. But now I wished I was back in my work dress and rag curlers. I didn't want him to look at me at all. He didn't deserve my efforts.

"Ben will propose this very night the way you look, Valynn. That material is just lovely, and you are beyond beautiful," Georgie said, smiling and hugging me close.

It wasn't what I wanted to hear at that moment. We heard a knock at the door and Georgie looked out the window to the front lawn.

"Ben is here," she said, smiling. "I am so happy you are giving him a chance tonight, Val. I do not think he would ever treat you badly like Niall McCray is," she said tenderly.

I nodded; I doubt any man would treat me like Niall McCray was. Suddenly I was nervous, nervous about being so close to Ben. I hadn't really spoken to him much since we were kids, and that had not ended well. I had gone for years disliking him because of the frogs. How would I endure an entire evening with him without hurting his feelings? I dreaded seeing Dr. McCray and Ava together, and I feared he might seek me out when I suddenly wanted him to stay away from me.

I heard Georgie greet Ben downstairs, and I sighed. "Just get through tonight, Valynn," I encouraged myself as I descended the stairs. I could do this, I was not one to back down from anything, and I would force myself to have fun.

Ben was in the parlor with Georgie and Keane, and when I walked in, the look on his face completely surprised me. Never, in my entire life, had a man looked at me like Ben was now. Not even Isaac after a year of courting. It was a precious look of revering me, cherishing me, how could I read it so easily?

My heart raced, and I found it melting in a strange sort of way right at Ben's feet. His warm brown eyes seemed to drink in the sight of me. His cheeks rose with color and his mouth smiled sweetly. He was genuinely pleased to see me, and my stomach fluttered.

He nervously took my hand in his. "Good heavens, Valynn! You took my breath away," he whispered for my ears only.

Suddenly, looking into his eyes, I found I could not breathe. This was Ben Weston, Ben from school, Frog Ben, the same Ben I had hardly noticed for years now. What was happening to me? He was still holding my hand, and I struggled to know what to do next. This was suddenly uncharted territory for me.

Georgie's eyes twinkled brightly as if she could feel what I was feeling at that very moment.

For the first time in my life, I was nearly afraid. "Thank you for escorting me tonight, Ben," I said softly.

His eyes twinkled and never left mine. Was I dreaming? It felt like it.

Keane cleared his throat and it seemed to wake me just a bit. "Would you mind helping me to greet the guests as they arrive out in the barn, Ben?" I asked timidly. Me? Timid? Oh no! *I was in trouble*.

Ben held my hand tenderly as we walked out to the barn. My hand had never felt this way before, so small, secure, and yet cherished. Yes, I was afraid now. "Wow! You have been busy; this place looks great, Valynn!" Ben said, smiling and taking in the decorations.

I thanked him softly, pleased he had noticed our hard work. His brown eyes twinkled in the lantern light; he was so very handsome dressed in an off white shirt and new denims. I nearly shook my head at the thought. Hadn't I been consumed in infatuation with Dr. McCray just half an hour ago?

"I can hardly believe I am here, with you," Ben whispered, squeezing my hand tenderly.

Oh! The flutters in my stomach soon reached my toes. I blushed just as Henry and Mormor walked in and greeted us excitedly.

Henry, Ben, and Keane began talking about the horses, and I turned my attention to straightening the table cloths. I could feel Ben's eyes following me with a gentle sort of warmth; it felt just like the blankets my mother warmed before the fireplace for us on cold nights. It enveloped me, comforted me, this new and strange warmth. Did he think I was pretty tonight in my new dress? Apparently he did. Had he truly told me I took his breath away? Frog Ben? How romantic he was! Where was Georgie? Where was Celia? I needed help and quickly. I was not one to fall for men's flattery, except my weakness where Dr. McCray had been concerned. But Ben was affecting my heart in a strange way, and I was quite confused. I found myself shocked and completely unprepared.

CHAPTER FOUR

The guests had begun to arrive, and I stood at Ben's side as we both greeted them, showing the musicians where to set up, showing women where to put their covered dishes, and showing parents where to drop the younger children off inside the house.

Ben was very outgoing and everyone seemed to like him. Why hadn't I ever noticed him before? Noticed how people took to him, listened to him. I watched with a new interest as women and men alike stopped and shook hands with him, talked to him, thanked him for helping with this or with that.

As if he could read my mind, he smiled at me tenderly, his brown eyes twinkling in the lantern light. I found myself holding my breath but in a good way.

My sister Celia and her husband John arrived. I quickly stole my nephew Johnny from her arms and showered him with kisses on his sweet auburn head.

"Genevieve and Augusta are inside the house. They will watch Johnny for you," I told my sister.

Celia smiled brightly and nodded to where Ben and John were conversing.

I could tell she wanted to know more of what was going on with Ben. I smiled and shrugged and then found myself blushing.

She looked giddy with excitement at the thought that I might like Ben Weston. I drew in a sharp breath, did I like Ben Weston? I had a scary feeling that I could. Just then, he took his place beside me, giving me that warm and excited feeling yet in a comfortable and pleasing way. I felt rather proud to be standing next to him. *Oh heavens!*

"Do you like children, Valynn?" he asked nervously.

I nodded and was relieved when my parents walked in, and I quickly rushed to greet them. I heard my father thank Ben again for the loads of wood and plead for him to take more money for the hard work it had taken to cut it, unload it, and stack it both times.

"No, no, Mr. Andley, I wanted to do it. Please, you paid me more than enough. I might need your help someday, so I may have to recall the favor," Ben insisted, and I marveled at how he had gently handled my father, leaving it as a favor to repay.

My father's eyes were bright as their talk turned to spring planting, and it made me feel warm inside knowing Ben worked hard, helped his neighbors, and seemed to get along with my father quite well. He had such an easy-going spirit about him, a servant's heart, that I could clearly see. They were good qualities in a man, I thought, smiling.

My mother looked at me knowingly, seeing the change in my heart towards my childhood nemesis. I felt these new and startling feelings on my cheeks, in a soft blush, as her blue eyes smiled at me. My parents liked Ben, and somehow, it endeared him to me even more.

My father reached out for my mother's hand as the music began to play. Ben joined me, standing very close to my side. I felt him take my hand in his, and our eyes met, just as Dr. McCray came in with Ava, nearly glued to his side. How could they even manage to walk so closely together, I wondered? It was a little intimately improper for being in public, and I doubted I could get a paper fan between the two of them.

Ben squeezed my hand tenderly in his. Did he know I had feelings for Dr. McCray or had thought I had feelings for Dr. McCray? I looked up into Ben's brown eyes, and suddenly I could not remember what it even was that I felt for Dr. Niall McCray.

I smiled at Ben in realization, that in half an hour, he had somehow managed to take my mind completely off Niall McCray.

His brown eyes looked hopeful to me, and I found myself wishing I knew what he was thinking in that moment.

Someone cleared his throat, and I quickly turned and greeted Ava first and then civilly greeted Dr. McCray whose intense green eyes were quickly taking in Ben and me. It was almost as if he could see these new feelings I had. I did feel giddy and a strange elation. And somehow, looking at Niall McCray now, he nearly seemed to dampen my spirits.

"Oh, Valynn! It is so good to see you here with Ben. I am so ashamed at what Isaac did to you, leaving you like he did after leading you on for a year. We have all been so disappointed in him. I hope you have not suffered terribly," Ava said sweetly.

She wasn't being mean, or spiteful. It was just her elegant air that made her seem superior; I knew that. "I am doing just fine, Ava. I think Isaac and I were more friends than in love. It made it easier for us both, I believe," I said warmly.

I felt Ben stiffen beside me and worried that we might have offended him by speaking of my previous relationship with Isaac. Of course he knew I had courted Isaac. He and Isaac had been best friends for years now. I gently squeezed his hand, wanting him to know that I was happy I was with him tonight. His twinkling brown eyes whispered that he appreciated my gesture.

I turned to find Dr. McCray looking me up and down as if I were on display, and it made me quite nervous and nearly ill feeling. It truly wasn't proper for him to ogle me in public like this. I felt myself leaning closer in to Ben.

Ava lifted her chin high with a scowl as if she too noticed his inappropriate glances and then rushed to greet Eleanor and Celia.

Dr. McCray nodded to Ben civilly but looked back to me. I didn't care for the look he was giving me. It was nothing like the look Ben had given me as I walked down the stairs. It was missing something. Why had I allowed myself to get attached to him? To even seek his attention?

"You are breathtaking tonight, Valynn," he said, causing me to blush. He had just said the same thing Ben had, but somehow, the sincerity in Ben's voice, and mostly in his eyes, seemed more endearing to me. Dr. McCray had no right to say such things to me. And how dare the man say such a thing in front of my escort?

I felt Ben Stiffen beside me and lean in closer. Oh heavens, the barn was getting warm this night!

"She is breathtaking. And tonight, she is my date, so I will thank you to take your flirtations back to Ava," Ben said firmly, causing my heart to race.

I had not expected Ben to be possessive, but somehow I felt I had an ally for the evening. They both stood with tension swirling between them. Surely they wouldn't fight?

Thankfully, the music began, and with the mischievous grin that used to make my heart flutter, Dr. McCray walked off, only this time my heart did not flutter at his smile and flirtations. I merely felt relief as I watched him pull Ava close, very close. I suddenly knew that was all his intentions had ever been towards me, to flirt and to toy with my emotions. *I felt like such a fool.*

"Please forgive me for that, Valynn. May I have this dance?" I heard Ben ask sweetly.

I smiled and nodded, thankful for his diverting my stung pride and growing temper towards Dr. McCray.

Ben's strong arm went around my waist as he whirled me onto the dance floor. The pace of the dance was quite fast, and I laughed with pure joy as we whirled in and out of my friends and family as they danced. Ben was a wonderful dancer and very easy to look at. I couldn't stop smiling at him. His brown eyes were so sincere, warm, and held a cute little mixture of mischief in them. It made me want to know him more and to look at him more for certain. I could still see the boy I knew as a child, and yet there was more to him now, *much more*.

He looked as disappointed as I felt when the music ended and my brother-in-law John asked for the next dance. "I had a feeling this would happen," he said, still holding my hand.

"What?" I asked breathlessly.

"Fighting to dance with the prettiest girl in all of Lowe County."

John slapped his back playfully, and I smiled. I could say nothing, for he literally took my breath away. My eyes followed him to the refreshment table, and I was thankful he hadn't asked another girl to dance. I had enjoyed being in Ben's arms. I still couldn't believe it. Who knew Frog Ben could be so charming?

I danced the next half hour with my father, my brother-in-law Keane, Dr. Anderson, Dr. Childers, and then Ben's oldest brother Drew. I was enjoying the evening immensely and liked the fluttery feeling in my stomach when I would look for Ben and find him watching me with a gentle smile.

A waltz began to play, and I felt a rush of excitement as Ben hurried towards me to claim his dance. "I told you I would have to fight for your dances tonight," he whispered close to my ear.

I smiled and laughed. I was having such a good time. The waltz required Ben to hold me closer than the other dances, and I found myself quite nervous as he smiled down at me, his arm tightly around my waist, my left arm on his shoulder, and my right hand clasped in his.

"I am thankful I got to you for this slow one," he said with his brown eyes twinkling in the lantern light.

Oh! There went my stomach again. I was blushing profusely now. I was enjoying Ben's company more than I had ever dreamt was possible. "Do you remember when we were children, and we went to the creek and you found those tree frogs?" I asked softly as I smiled.

This time, he blushed, and it looked quite attractive on him. He squeezed my side tenderly and shook his head. "Oh, Valynn, I have prayed you had forgotten that was me," he confessed, smiling back at me.

I pretended to be serious. "Oh no, I have not forgotten, Ben Weston. I am terrified of frogs to this day!" I said, trying to keep from laughing. But it was true!

He bit his lip and watched my face, waiting for me to laugh, I suppose. "Well then, how can I make it up to you?" he asked, smiling and taking my breath with him. "I know! Allow me to come and court you, Valynn, and I will protect you from such fearsome creatures, for all your life... if you will let me," he said so sweetly, catching me off guard.

Had he just asked to court me? My mind whirled, my heart raced, and the room began to spin as fast as the couples dancing next to us.

"I am sorry to say it so sudden like that. But I have waited for so long now. Forgive me if I spoke too soon," he said tenderly as his eyes looked a bit defeated.

I shook my head no. I couldn't think. I was overwhelmed in a strange and wonderful way. Oh heavens! "It isn't that. It *was* unexpected, but not in a bad way," I said, struggling to bring back that twinkle in his eyes.

"Could we go outside, just for a breath of fresh air?" he asked softly.

The song had just come to an end, and I nodded my agreement as he took my hand in his and walked me outside.

It was cold, and I immediately shivered although the crisp air felt inviting. The moon was full, and the sky was filled with stars. Music played in the background, and it made a most romantic setting.

"Shall I go for your coat?" Ben asked nervously.

I shook my head no and hugged my arms to me. We walked to the fence surrounding the stables, and I looked up to the heavens, all brilliant in its nightly glory. Something was changing in me and so suddenly. Hours ago, I thought I would always love Niall McCray. But now I wondered if I ever had.

"I love to watch the stars at night." I looked over and smiled at Ben's confession. "My dog Yonder and I sit on the back porch every night, watching the stars and moon, the herds of deer as they walk to the pond for a drink," he said wistfully.

I smiled. "You and Yonder? What sort of a name is Yonder?" I asked, laughing.

He smiled. "When I found him, the only command he seemed to understand was 'Go fetch it over yonder.' I laughed again. "It just sort of stuck, I suppose," he laughed.

He looked nearly beautiful in the moonlight if one dared to call a man such a thing. I suddenly wondered what it would be like to hug him. He was such a large and strong man. He made me feel safe, cherished. I sighed. We hadn't resumed our talk of courting, and I wondered if Ben would have the nerve to ask again?

"So, just you and Yonder, huh?" I asked, baiting him. I looked back up to the stars, biting my lip for I truly couldn't stop smiling. Did I want to court Ben Weston? Oh heavens, it didn't sound bad at all!

"Yes, just me and Yonder. It gets lonely some times," he admitted.

For some reason, those words melted my heart.

"Valynn, I have rehearsed this night in my mind for over a year now. And I have made a mess of things," Ben said with a tender smile.

My heart raced at his admission. "You have?" I asked, surprised.

He nodded as he looked up to the night sky as if he could find his words written there. "I was planning to ask you if I could court you over a year ago. I was waiting for your seventeenth birthday." He was uncomfortable confessing this to me, and yet, I could sense he was determined to say more.

"But you didn't ask me," I stated softly.

He shook his head no.

"Did something change your mind?" I didn't know why I was trying to help him along; perhaps my curiosity was getting the best of me. I wanted to know what had happened, what had changed, and I was freezing now.

"Isaac did. The day of your party, Isaac told me he had spoken with your father and received his blessing to court you. I was devastated. But Isaac was my friend." He took a deep breath.

I suddenly realized how brave Ben was for telling me this now. It took a lot of courage, and it made his words mean so much more to me, knowing he spoke them from his heart.

"I tried to get over you, but I failed. When Isaac told me he was leaving to search the gold mines, I told him he was a fool. If I was ever lucky enough to court you, I would never leave you, not for a day," he whispered tenderly.

My heart nearly stopped. Was this not the kind of love I had told Isaac I wished for? Just like Keane and Georgie had? How had I not seen this affection in Ben before tonight? My heart raced wildly. "Ben," was all I could whisper in return. I was overwhelmed with such shocking emotion, and it felt so pure and so right.

"Valynn, I have prayed and fasted about asking you to court. I ask that you do the same, and then give me your answer. I do not want to rush you in any way. But I know several men who are interested in you, and I have to admit my fear in losing you again," he said softly.

My heart ached to know he had been hurting for a year, watching as Isaac courted me. And I had never known. I shivered, and he sighed as he took my hands in his. He was so warm and so wonderful. He had prayed and fasted. His intent was pure, right. It was all I could do not to kiss those sweet cheeks of his.

"Will you pray about it, Valynn?" he asked anxiously.

I nodded.

He sighed in relief, and yet he looked anything but relieved. "Let's get you inside," he urged.

"Valynn!" I heard and startled.

I whirled around to find Dr. McCray behind us. "What is it, Dr. McCray?" I asked with my heart racing. I was suddenly angry that he had dared to break such a beautiful moment between Ben and me.

"Are you all right out here, with him?" he asked in his arrogant way.

I gasped, and Ben stiffened. "Of course I am all right. Ben is a gentleman, and we were just talking," I said in Ben's defense.

"Don't be out here long, or your reputation will suffer. Mr. Weston should know this," Dr. McCray hissed.

"I would never do anything to dishonor, Valynn," Ben said, becoming angry.

I quickly took Ben's hand back in my own; I could feel him trembling with anger. Dr. McCray walked back inside with a dark scowl.

"Forget him, Ben. He is a miserable sort of fellow," I whispered.

"He is in love with you, Valynn," Ben sighed.

My heart stopped for a second. Surely he was wrong. I looked into Ben's eyes and I shook my head no. "No, he doesn't love me. He may love women in general, but he cares for Ava," I assured him.

He smiled weakly. "He *is* in love with you, Valynn, *but so am I*. I won't rush you, but I hope you will pray about letting me court you," Ben whispered, kissing my knuckles and making my knees feel weak.

Ben, wonderful Ben, standing so close I could smell his cologne and fresh laundered shirt. He had prayed and fasted about his future wife. He had been in love with me for over a year. Ben Weston, Frog Ben, and I had never known until this night. It was as if the moment was destined by a greater power. I had never felt such peace, or so cherished. "I will pray about it, Ben," I assured him.

He nodded, and led me back inside.

Genevieve immediately pulled me into a group dance, and I turned to see Ben watching me with a tender look on his face. I smiled brightly to encourage him. I didn't understand what was happening this night, and it was all I could do not to run to Ben and tell him 'yes', that he could come courting me.

He smiled mischievously, and I shook my head in amazement. Who would have guessed I could fall for Ben Weston, the pain in the backside, Frog Ben? But I suddenly realized I was; I was falling for Ben... and pretty fast.

I was dancing with Dr. Anderson once again when Dr. McCray cut in.

I gasped at the boldness of the man and shook my head at him as he took me in his arms possessively. Looking into those green eyes that I had recently felt lost in, I could now only feel anger. Dr. McCray forced me to see a side of myself that I didn't like, a naïve and gullible side, and I hated the intimidation and vulnerability I felt in his presence. His anger toward me was apparent, but I couldn't think past my own disapproval of him. "That was quite rude," I said angrily as I watched Dr. Anderson hang his head and walk off to the side.

Dr. McCray frowned. "You are avoiding me tonight, Valynn," he accused.

I raised my chin high and shook my head no. "I came with Ben; he is my escort. He *asked me* to the dance," I said truthfully.

"Yes, you and Ben are looking quite cozy together. Do you let every man who takes you outside kiss your hand?" he asked, irritated with me.

My own eyes sought his, and I prayed he could see how angry I was with him. "It was merely a kiss to my hand. How about you and Ava; did she sew your pant leg to her skirt? A feather couldn't fit between the two of you!" I hissed.

His face was beyond red now. "Jealous still? Really, Valynn, is that what this is about? Coming with Ben, driving me insane with jealously, because you are jealous?" he growled.

His hands tightened on my arms and it nearly hurt, and nearly scared me. If I hadn't been in a room of people who loved me, I would have been quite afraid. I shook my head as I searched his face. "I am not jealous," I stated honestly. I could see the truth so clearly this night. I had dreaded seeing them together, but I wasn't jealous this night, not anymore.

My eyes searched for Ben, for he had changed everything. He stood stiff, watching us like a hawk watched her baby. I smiled tenderly at Ben, sensing he was worried about my feelings toward Dr. McCray, but it only proved to provoke Niall all the more.

"You know you're attracted to me. Admit it. You only came with Ben to hurt me!" he insisted.

I shook my head no. "I came with Ben because he asked me. He wanted to spend this evening with me and me alone!" I couldn't believe the nerve of this man!

"You know I wanted to come with you! I told you not all things were as they seemed. You didn't have to try and hurt me, Valynn! It was hard enough on me, not being with you," he whispered too close to my cheek and ear.

I tried to move back just a little in his arms, but he held me firmly. I looked at him incredulously. "Who I come with is none of your concern! I did not try to hurt you! You have no claim on me, Dr. McCray!" I said angrily and a little more than frightened.

"It *is* my concern, Valynn! Do not tell me that it is not!"

I felt my heart pounding loudly. I had never been around an angry man in my entire life. "You have no right," I hissed.

"And Ben does?" he asked, getting even more riled.

"Ben is different...," I began, but he cut me off quickly.

"Oh yes, Ben is different. I apologize. Ben is an honest man. I imagine after kissing your hand and risking your reputation, he will feel obligated to court you now," he said with a smirk that I longed to slap off his face.

My cheeks burned crimson and I gritted my teeth. "Ben kissed my hand just after he asked me to court him," I said, watching his handsome face fall into what appeared to be despair.

He stared at me long and hard, and my eyes never left his. The tension was high, and his eyes did not reveal the true goodness and tenderness that I saw when I looked into Ben's eyes. The realization was so strong. "And just what was your reply?" he asked me softly, surprising me since I still saw anger in his eyes, and I truly wondered why.

"That is none of your affair, Dr. McCray! For weeks you have flirted with me, dangled my heart around, not caring if you hurt me. Ben is in love with me and he wants to court me and me alone. You are a grown man who cannot discern his own heart and yet toys with the naïve hearts of others," I hissed, angry at myself for once thinking I was falling in love with such a rake.

"Come outside with me, Valynn," he bid me, but I quickly shook my head no.

I started to panic. Dr. McCray was beyond angry, I could tell. I wouldn't dare.

"Please, I must speak with you before you make a big mistake. You must hear me out on this," he pleaded.

"No. I will not!" I said firmly, just as the music ended.

To my relief, Ben was immediately beside me, taking my hand just as Dr. McCray let go of it. Their eyes met, and I feared a fight. "Are you all right, Valynn?" I heard Ben ask as he watched Dr. McCray with a scowl, for the doctor was still standing before me, watching me, his eyes pleading with me.

I could hardly breathe. "Yes, Ben. Thank you," I said, holding his hand a bit tighter and praying he did not let go of me.

Ben escorted me for a glass of punch, and I sighed deeply, trying to calm my nerves and regain the magical wonder the night had held earlier before that despicable man had danced with me.

A slow waltz played once more, and Ben softly asked me to dance.

I smiled and allowed him to lead me to the dance floor. Dr. McCray and Ava had stepped outside over half an hour ago, and I prayed they had left for good.

Ben pulled me closely, and it felt like heaven. I smiled brightly. "Your conversation with Dr. McCray seemed tense."

And my smile faded. I shrugged.

"Are you certain you are all right, Valynn?"

I nodded as Ben's eyes searched my face. He was so sweet and caring. I squeezed the large muscle of his arm where my hand lay as we danced. I felt safe in his arms. Content. I would be happy if I only danced with Ben the rest of the night or for the rest of my life. Oh heavens! Where had that thought come from? I swallowed hard. I had never felt this way before, not even with Isaac. I suddenly didn't want this night to end. "I am having a wonderful time tonight, Ben," I said softly as I smiled and looked up into those warm eyes of his. A girl could get lost in eyes like that, and I suddenly wished I could.

Ben smiled. "I am glad, Valynn. I like to see you happy. You are beautiful every day, but tonight, you glow," he whispered.

I felt like I was glowing and falling even deeper for this man before me.

"I wondered when I might get to see you again. I could bring another load of wood over tomorrow… if it wasn't too soon, of course."

I had to laugh, for he was truly too sweet. "Ben Weston, how do you have any wood left?" I teased.

He blushed. "There will always be enough wood if it means I can see you again."

His words were so soft and tender. So sincere. Tears filled my eyes, but they were happy tears. "Cutting wood is hard work, Ben Weston." Why would he think he had to bring my father wood if he wanted to see me?

"It is worth it to me, Valynn. Only say I can see you again," he whispered with that mischievous light in his eyes.

Oh heavens I wanted to kiss him! "Would you like to come for supper, Ben?" I asked nervously. This was so unlike me.

He smiled and nodded.

"At seven?" I asked.

He sighed. "Seven is a mighty long time to wait, but yes, I will be there, thank you, Valynn."

I could only nod for my emotions ran too strong.

"Do you think I could drive you home tonight?" he asked.

I smiled and bit my bottom lip. I felt the same way, and it was so very strange and so very wonderful all at the same time. "I am sorry, Ben. I am supposed to spend the night with Georgiana again." I hated the disappointed look on his face. "But I will see you tomorrow night for supper, and if you are a good boy, there might be pie!" I said, trying to make him smile again. It worked and my stomach fluttered wildly at his smile.

"I do like pie," he said, blushing.

And I liked him! *Truly liked him!*

Ben stayed and helped us to pick things up. Georgie and I would finish most of the cleaning on the morrow. He seemed hesitant to leave me although everyone else had gone home except for my parents. I found I didn't want him to leave either. "I guess this is it, until tomorrow then," he said softly.

I nodded, and my heart did a small somersault inside my chest as he took my hands in his.

"Gosh, this is hard," he said.

I felt the warmth of my blush on my cheeks and smiled. I was falling in love with this man, and I was suddenly certain no one else would do. "Ben, did you really mean it? Do you really want to court me?" I asked nervously.

He smiled so tenderly and nodded. "I have never been more certain of anything," he said, searching my eyes in hope.

I felt like bawling like a baby. But in a good way. "Well, Ben Weston, you had better go and ask my father for permission, I suppose, if you really mean it," I said, smiling coyly. But in truth, I could hardly breathe.

Ben's eyes searched mine, and he smiled, surprised. "Do you mean it, Valynn? You will let me come and court you?" he asked.

I nodded, my heart soaring like it never had before. "Yes, Ben, I am certain, so very certain," I said emotionally.

He kissed my knuckles again and rushed toward my father.

My mother smiled, and Georgiana stood watching from across the barn with her mouth open in shock.

I shrugged and then giggled, covering my blushing cheeks with my cool hands. I had no idea what on earth had happened this night, but somehow, my future had just changed drastically, and I was happier than I had ever been.

"What is this about Ben Weston, Val? Did you truly give him permission to speak with me about courting you?" my father asked with a grin. He was happy with the idea, I could clearly see.

I smiled and squeezed his shoulder. He had pulled me into the house to speak to me alone and now I awaited his answer. "Yes, Father! I cannot quite believe it myself, but tonight, everything has changed. Ben came, and I don't know, my heart started racing. He says such sweet things. He is a good man, Father, and he cares for me. I am so happy and so surprised," I said with a nervous giggle and with tears filling my eyes.

My dad chuckled and smiled. "Ben is a good man, and he can provide a good life for you, Val. Of course you have my blessing. And you are right- he does care for you, it is clear to see by the smile on his face. It warms my heart, Val," he said.

I laughed as I wiped away a stray tear. What was happening to me? I never cried! "Oh Father! Thank you! He has been praying and fasting, and I shall do the same, but I feel it is right. I cannot explain it, other than I just feel such a peace, and it feels so pure and right," I said, shaking my head in wonder. "Oh, wonderful! I shall not be able to stop crying now," I said, wiping my eyes again.

My father hugged me closely. "That is what love is, Valynn. It is pure and right, and in its presence, you will feel at peace. But, I must ask you, Val, what about Dr. McCray? It was just yesterday you talked of him. I know you had decided not to allow him to court you, but I could see your heart was leaning towards him although I admit it worried me some," father said softly.

I sighed. "Up until tonight, I struggled with my feelings for him. He is always flirting with me but then runs to Ava. He knows I am attracted to him, but I do not see the sincerity and goodness in his eyes that I saw for the first time tonight in Ben's. After dancing with Ben for only an hour, I found myself wondering what I ever saw in Dr. McCray. The way I feel for Ben is so different, even more different than what I felt with Isaac. It is exciting, but in a good and pure way as if this is it, as if I have found where I am supposed to be. Does that make sense, Father?" I asked, needing his wisdom.

My father smiled tenderly. "It does, Valynn. And I know you pray daily about staying in God's will. Perhaps Dr. McCray was just merely an attraction, perhaps even a diversion. I think you have been wise with your decisions not to court Dr. McCray. If a man is in love, he cannot bear to be with anyone else but the girl he loves. It has bothered me greatly that he flirts with you and goes to Ava. Ben would never do such a thing," my father said with a tender smile.

I shook my head no. "Ben is a good man. I want to court him, Father. I have been so happy getting to know him tonight. I think I am already falling in love with him," I confessed.

My father smiled brightly. "Good, because Ben asked if I would force him into a long courtship; he doesn't think he can wait much longer to marry you."

I thought I saw tears glistening in his eyes. I bit my lip, nervous and excited and then laughed. Ben Weston loved me, and I knew at that moment, I was truly falling in love with him as well.

I walked out into the darkness with only the lights from the kitchen glowing dimly.

Keane said goodnight to Ben and left us alone.

Ben twirled his hat in his hands nervously. "I suppose I had best head home now before Keane runs me off," he chuckled.

I smiled, for I felt the same way. Tomorrow night seemed too far away. I didn't want Ben to leave. I was afraid I would wake and find this all a dream.

"Valynn, I am so happy," he whispered.

I smiled and nodded. "I am happy, too, Ben," I confessed with my heart racing.

"Good night, Valynn. Sweet dreams," he whispered.

I had rather hoped he might kiss me, now that we were courting. But he just nodded and climbed onto his horse. "Good night, Ben. Ride safely," I said, hugging myself lest I rush to him and embarrass myself by kissing him.

I watched him ride away, knowing that somehow, in one evening, Ben Weston had changed my life forever. *And I couldn't wait for our forever to begin.*

CHAPTER FIVE

"Valynn Clarice Andley! What is going on?" Georgie asked, smiling with her hands on her hips.

I leaned back against the kitchen door and smiled brightly. Watching Keane's and my sister's faces as they waited for my explanation caused me to burst into nervous laughter. "I cannot tell you for certain, but it seems I am courting Ben Weston, and I think I must be falling in love," I laughed.

Both their mouths opened in surprise. "Val, truly?" Georgie asked, rushing to me and hugging me closely.

I couldn't seem to stop smiling. "Can you come up later and talk with me?" I asked in a whisper.

She leaned back and smiled. "Try and stop me," she promised.

"Girls!" Keane said, shaking his head and leaving the room.

Georgie and I both burst into giggles.

We lay in the featherbed upstairs at Kenrick Farms, my sister Georgie and I. I relayed all the romantic events of the night, the surprise in my heart's awakening to Ben Weston, the sweet things he had said to me, and the happiness I now felt. I couldn't explain just how right and pure this feeling was. I had never felt this way before. We giggled, we cried, and then we lay whispering of the future and just what it might hold.

"Val, I am so happy for you and Ben. I was concerned a little about Dr. McCray. I like Niall, but it didn't seem he was being honorable towards you," she confided.

I sighed and nodded. "He came outside and accused Ben of risking my reputation. Then he rudely cut in on Dr. Anderson, accused me of avoiding him all evening, and was quite angry to learn Ben had asked to court me. Somehow, he feels as if I am his concern. He nearly frightened me," I said, still wondering how Dr. McCray felt he had any right to feel anything towards me or Ben. He had time and again chosen Ava Stein.

"What did he do to you?" she demanded, that motherly intuition kicking in.

"He held my arms rather tightly. But it was the look in his eyes that bothered me the most, I suppose. He said I was trying to make him jealous by using Ben. He accused me of trying to hurt him on purpose."

"Of all the nerve!" Georgie said, shaking her head. I nodded. "He most certainly is a devil, Valynn! You would do good to stay away from him," she warned.

I would stay away from him. Far away from him!

"Oh Georgie, I have never felt this way, in all of my life. Niall did make me feel thrilled, excited, but there was that uneasiness there that wouldn't let me enjoy my feelings. But Ben, he is so different. All I could think of was how much I wished he would kiss me. He makes me feel so treasured and safe. It is going to be a horridly long day tomorrow, waiting for supper, waiting on Ben."

Georgie giggled, and I smiled. I doubted if I would sleep this night. Was Ben and Yonder sitting on their porch, thinking of me?

Georgie kissed my cheek goodnight and tucked me in, just as she had when I was a little girl.

I doused the lamp and lay in the darkness, thanking God for sending Ben Weston to me all those years ago but especially for sending him to me this night.

It was a few hours before dawn when I heard a loud knocking on the front door of the farmhouse. I sat up, trying to wake and determine if I had heard the door or if I was dreaming. Again, a loud pounding at the door reverberated through the house, and now a loud voice calling out for me.

My heart raced, and I was a little more than afraid as I heard Keane rushing through the house. Jori was now awake and crying. I quickly tied on my robe and slipped my feet into my slippers.

"Not now, Niall, go home! Have you been drinking?" I heard Keane ask, and I gasped. What was Dr. McCray doing here; it was three in the morning!

"I have to see Valynn; please, I know she is here," I heard him say more calmly.

Jori continued to cry, and I heard Keane threaten to beat the tar out of Dr. McCray if he didn't leave.

I quickly rushed down the stairs and heard Keane call to me. "Valynn, go to your room. Niall is in no shape to see you," Keane said angrily.

"Please, Keane, I beg of you, you may stay right beside her. I would never harm her in any way. But I must speak with her! Please!" Dr. McCray pleaded with such urgency that it frightened me. He was disheveled and looked tormented. He didn't appear in a hurry to leave.

"I will speak with him," I heard myself say nervously. "But Keane will stay with me," I said, continuing down the stairs on trembling legs, my eyes searching Dr. McCray's haunted green ones. "Niall, what on earth are you doing here?" I asked concerned, for he hardly even looked like himself.

He led me into the parlor, and I sat down on the sofa, he in a chair across from me with Keane standing closely behind him.

I gasped as I smelled spirits on him. "You are toasted!" I accused.

Niall hung his head in shame. I had never seen him anything but well groomed. He was a mess. "Valynn, I cannot continue on like this. I have been living in torment without you. *I love you*," Dr. McCray said, shocking me.

I shook my head, but he held his hand up for me to allow him to continue.

"I do! I tried not to, I did, but it is no use. I cannot get you out of my head! I want you to marry me, run away with me, tonight, now!" he pleaded desperately.

I heard Keane swear behind him, and I gasped. "What?" I asked, knowing I could not have heard him correctly.

He reached out and took my hands in his, but I quickly pulled away. He was frightening me. "You have feelings for me, I know you do. I want you to marry me, tonight! I cannot wait another day! We will leave Crawford, make our home in a new town. Just say yes! Say you will go with me. I love you desperately, Valynn," he said with such emotion, I again felt the uneasy feeling I had experienced when around him before.

Something wasn't right; I could feel it. I had waited for weeks now, just for him to decide he liked me, not Ava, and suddenly, he wished to marry me? Why now? Why leave? "Run away? Why? Why leave Crawford?" I asked out loud, trying to figure this all out.

He sighed and shook his head. "I want to start over; I want time for just us with no interruptions," he said, running his hands through his dark hair.

He looked distraught as if he struggled with his inner self somehow. When Ben told me he loved me, his brown eyes revealed his love, they twinkled with affection, and his words had been sweet and endearing. But Dr. McCray's declarations had me frightened, and I realized clearly, I felt no love for him at all. "I cannot. I do not believe you know what true love is. I am courting Ben, and I have feelings for him," I confessed.

Dr. McCray raised his head and looked angry. Keane moved forward. "I said I will not harm her, Keane," he growled.

I shivered.

"You just danced with him, Valynn, it isn't love, and you have feelings for me. I know you do. And *I* cannot go on without you. *You* are driving me insane; *you* are all I think of. Come with me, please! I know you can love me!" he begged.

I shook my head no. "No, Niall, I do not love you. I will not leave Crawford, and my family, especially for a man who would never stand up and court me properly, a man who never proved his affection was for me alone. I think you are merely jealous of Ben and are angry that you no longer have my attention," I said, growing angry myself. I stood on trembling legs.

Sensing that I was dismissing the doctor, Keane headed toward the front door to see him out.

Suddenly, Dr. McCray pulled me to his chest; his eyes searched mine before lowering his mouth to mine and kissing me hard and passionately. It was as if he was possessed and only I could save him. His kiss was intense, demanding, and I shoved him off just as Keane yanked him backwards and punched him in the nose.

I screamed out, and Keane lifted Niall to his feet by his collar. "Get out of my house! And do not ever go near Valynn again, do you hear me?" Keane asked angrily.

"What on earth?" Georgie asked, frightened in the doorway.

"I am sorry, Valynn, I love you! Please forgive me, but I love you. I had to show you, I had to prove to you, I love you! I do! Please come with me. *I need you!*" Niall pleaded with me again, blood gushing from his nose.

My knees threatened to buckle beneath me, and my heart raced in fear as I took in the torment in his eyes. I shook my head no. "I will not go with you, Dr. McCray," I said softly.

He bowed his head in defeat and then quickly apologized to Keane and Georgie and asked their forgiveness. He turned to look back at me, his face so torn and filled with pain.

I didn't realize I was crying until Keane shut and locked the door behind Niall.

Georgie rushed to me and hugged me closely. "Did he hurt you?" she asked, concerned.

I shook my head no and wept on her shoulder. "He kissed me, that is all," I whispered.

"He is out of his head, Valynn. He is a good man, but he made a bad choice in coming here like this," Keane said softly.

I nodded and thanked Keane. My legs trembled as I climbed the stairs to bed.

Georgie insisted on sleeping next to me once she rocked Jori back to sleep. She placed her in bed between us, and I smiled as I looked at her sweet angelic face.

"He must love you something fierce to come here like he did," she whispered.

I shook my head no. "It isn't love, not a love I want anyways. It was a desperate attempt to keep me. He just doesn't want Ben to have me," I said, certain of it.

She nodded. "Why did he think you would run away with him? We would have fought him tooth and nail to keep you in Crawford," she said, sighing.

The entire episode was strange, and I found I could hardly wait to go home. I was frightened of Niall. And I hated my fear. I hated that I had ever flirted with him and dreamt of a future with him. I just prayed he left me alone now.

I spent the day helping Georgie clean up after the dance and putting the barn back in order. My heart was heavy after Dr. McCray's disturbing visit. I tried to think of Ben, to recapture the magical feelings I had only hours ago, but it seemed as if my fear outweighed the joy that I had found the night before.

I was exhausted and my nerves frazzled by the time Keane drove me home that afternoon. I truly didn't need the escort, but he insisted that he wasn't taking any chances of Dr. McCray, hiding in wait for me.

I knew now, that what I felt towards Dr. McCray was mere physical attraction, and even that had diminished greatly after his forcing his kiss on me. I knew that he hadn't meant it to harm me, that it was desperation, and more than likely that the spirits he had consumed had caused him to kiss me like that.

But it did bother me… greatly. Even after courting Isaac for a year, I had never been kissed like that before. It angered me that he had taken that piece of innocence from me without asking. His haunted and tormented eyes frightened me. His arrogance and lack of self-control intimidated me. I prayed that I wouldn't have to see him again for a very long time.

Over a cup of hot cocoa, I told my parents what Dr. McCray had done. My father was angry with him, and my mother shook her head in disappointment. "He must be very much in love with you, Valynn," she said softly.

"It isn't love, it is lust! Look at how he treats her, Margaret. He flirts with her but doesn't court her; he spends time with another woman and then goes crazy with jealously when he sees Ben care for her. And then forces himself on her right in front of Keane. I am thankful our son-in-law busted Niall's nose good. If I had been there I would have made certain he had two black eyes as well," my father said, shaking his head.

I smiled weakly. My father was taking this harder than I. "I am all right now. And I am anxious to put this behind me and see Ben tonight," I said, kissing both my parents on the cheek.

"Go on up and rest, Valynn. You need a good nap before Ben comes. Genevieve can help with supper tonight," Mother urged me.

I nodded. I was mentally and physically exhausted.

But my sleep only brought haunting dreams of Niall McCray's desperate green eyes searching for me, his desperate voice calling for me in the dark. I was more afraid of him now than ever.

"Are you going to marry Ben?" my youngest sister Augusta asked me.

I smiled. "He has only asked me to court him. Courting is a time to get to know one another, a time to see if we are compatible to marry," I said, smiling and pinching the end of her sweet little nose. At fifteen, Augusta was becoming a beauty.

"I heard Ben tell Drew that you were the most beautiful girl in the world," Genevieve said, giggling as she curled my hair for me.

I blushed. "He did?" I asked breathlessly.

She nodded. "I was following Millie, carrying Baby Will as she carried her empty dishes out to the wagon after the dance. Drew and Ben were in front of us and didn't realize we could hear them. He is in love with you," Genevieve said, giddy with sixteen-year-old excitement.

My heart raced, and I thought I might die before seven o'clock came. I turned to look at the clock on the bedside table; I still had half an hour to go.

"Ben Weston is much more handsome than Isaac Stein," Augusta said, choosing which dress she thought I should wear.

"Augusta!" I exclaimed in shock.

She merely blushed and grinned.

I took a deep breath and smiled. "He is isn't he?" I agreed.

Both of my sisters giggled.

I closed my eyes and enjoyed the feeling of Genevieve fixing my hair. It relaxed my anxious heart. Ben was truly more handsome than Isaac. How had I never seen it before? Perhaps I had been too caught up in being the next 'Stein Bride,' for all the girls in Lowe County wished to marry into the wealthy Stein family. And I had been one of them. But I didn't regret Isaac leaving, not at all. His leaving for gold was the best thing that could have happened to me. For now, I was courting Ben. Just the thought of it gave me a tingly delight. I rather liked falling in love.

Suddenly we heard a horse, and Augusta rushed to my bedroom window. "He is here early!" Augusta exclaimed, looking out my bedroom window.

I took in a deep breath and tried to calm my nerves. Would Ben feel the same for me this evening as he did the last? I prayed he would. So much had happened since the dance last evening. I worried that it had been a dream and that somehow Dr. McCray had ruined it all.

I smoothed down my dress of burgundy muslin and looked in the mirror and frowned at my puffy dark eyes. Hopefully the dim lighting in the parlor would hide the apparent truth that I had been troubled.

I walked into the parlor where my mother had served Ben a mug of hot coffee to warm him from his ride, and to my relief, the same brown eyes that had twinkled with affection the night before, now twinkled beautifully once again.

"Valynn, it is good to see you," Ben said, standing to his feet. His cheeks were rosy from the cold and his warm smile graced his handsome face.

I suddenly had the urge to throw myself into his arms and weep with relief, but of course I refrained. I didn't want to scare him off so soon. "Ben," I could only manage to get out as we stared into one another's eyes.

My father cleared his throat and told me to escort Ben into the dining room.

We both blushed, and I reached out and nervously took Ben's hand in mine. I was again overwhelmed by how warm and wonderful it felt to hold his hand. He smiled tenderly as I led him in to sit down beside me at the table.

I found I was quite nervous eating next to Ben and merely picked at my supper which was not like me at all.

My family watched with smiles, knowing that I was a hearty eater most of the time.

My father and Ben spoke of the upcoming planting season and cattle prices. I watched my father's face, and I was pleased to see he clearly thought highly of Ben and his ability to run a farm.

I found myself wondering about Ben's farm, what the house looked like, the yard. I didn't care, mind you, truly he could live in a dugout at this point, and I would surely follow him with no complaints. I smiled; I didn't even feel like myself anymore, *I felt better*.

After supper, Mother announced Ben and I could retire with our dessert into the parlor, and Augusta and

Genevieve would stay in the dining room with my parents. I was used to this arrangement from when I had courted Isaac. Although he had only come twice a week to court, we normally played games with my family when he was visiting.

We both sat on the sofa and placed our chocolate cake on the table before us.

"I hope you had a good day today," I said, nervously trying to break the awkward silence between us.

Ben smiled and blushed as he reached over and took my hand.

My cheeks felt warm as I looked into his eyes.

"I think it has been the longest day of my life. I thought tonight would never get here," he confessed with a gentle wink.

I couldn't hide my smile at his admission.

"This sounds silly, but, I was afraid by the time I arrived tonight, I would find you had changed your mind about letting me court you," he confessed.

His nervousness made him all the more handsome to me. It was refreshing after being subjected to Dr. McCray's overly confident disposition. "I have been worried that perhaps it was all a dream, that when you arrived, you wouldn't want to court me after all," I said, squeezing his hand tenderly.

He smiled. "Aww, Valynn! There is no fear of that," he said, breathless and causing me to blush. He looked down at our joined hands and cleared his throat. "There is… something…. I feel I need to ask you. You may tell me it is none of my affair. I laid awake most of the night, concerned over this," he sighed.

"What is it?" I encouraged. Fear crept into my heart and soul.

"Well, it is about Dr. McCray. I know we talked a little about him last night. I still believe he is in love with you. I couldn't help but notice how much he seems to affect you," he said softly. "I just have to know, for my heart is already lost to you, Valynn. I cannot pursue courting you if you have any feelings for him at all. It would crush me beyond repair, I am afraid," he whispered this last part.

I took in a deep breath, and his eyes looked fearful. "I did not believe Dr. McCray was in love with me. But, you were right, he is. He came back to Kenrick Farms this morning at three o'clock and woke the entire house. He was distraught, and I was a little frightened, I must admit." I said, nervously folding my handkerchief into tiny squares over and over.

"Keane tried to send him away, but he was insistent he speak with me. He had Keane angry and Jori crying, so I consented to speak to him. I have never seen a man look so haunted, so tormented as Dr. McCray did. And I still haven't a clue why. I still do not understand it all. But he started confessing his love for me, telling me he couldn't live without me. And then he begged me to run away with him and marry him, right then and there. To start over some place new. It didn't make sense, and I knew I didn't love him, so I told him no. I told him I had no feelings for him and that I cared for you. He begged and pleaded, but I refused him. When he went to leave, he grabbed me to him and….," I couldn't finish. I was embarrassed to have had that kiss stolen, a passionate kiss that only my future husband had been entitled to, not Niall McCray.

"What? Valynn, what did he do?" Ben asked, getting angry. "Did he hurt you? I will kill him..," Ben began, hurt and angry, but I quickly interrupted him.

"No, he did not hurt me, not physically anyway. He kissed me until Keane pulled him back and bloodied his nose," I said.

Ben stood from the sofa and began to pace in front of the fireplace. I could see this news hurt him, just as it had hurt me and my family.

"He seemed to come to his senses after being punched in the nose, and he apologized to me and to Keane and Georgie. I think he understands now, and I do not think he will try anything else," I said, trying to encourage Ben, trying to get that sparkle back into his brown eyes.

Ben seemed lost and forlorn, and my heart ached at having told him anything at all. But I knew he deserved to know; I had to be honest. But perhaps I had once again spoken when I should have been silent; yes, it was always my downfall.

"Ben, I didn't tell you this to make you angry," I said softly.

Ben stopped pacing and stood before the fireplace, his face softened. "I know, Valynn. I am angry at Dr. McCray, not at you. And I suppose I am jealous that he has done what I have only dreamt of, kissing you, asking you to marry," he said, so tenderly my heart melted.

Poor Ben, he looked like he was in agony. "Ben, please know that I have no feelings for Dr. McCray. In the beginning there had been an attraction. He had asked me to court him several times, but each time I denied him. He was also courting Ava Stein, and somehow I always felt a little uneasy around him. I felt intimidated in his presence, and I hated that feeling. But last night, it all changed. After dancing with you and talking with you, I was clearly able to see and feel the difference. You make me feel cherished, at peace with who I am. I never felt that way with Isaac or Dr. McCray," I said softly. My heart ached. I wanted so desperately to feel that magic again with Ben, to put all this confusion and anger behind us.

Ben gave me a weak smile. "I do cherish you, Valynn," he whispered. "I had better go now," he said, looking out the front parlor window.

He hadn't even eaten his cake. My heart sank. Ben was hurting, and now he was leaving. Once again Dr. McCray had ruined the pure and magical feelings Ben and I had shared. I found myself praying and repenting, for at that moment I hated Niall McCray.

I fell into a sort of melancholy over the next few days. A large snowstorm came in with a vengeance, and I found myself restlessly floating about the house, wishing I could be with Georgie at Kenrick Farms. But I feared I might run into Dr. McCray if I dared go.

I had not heard from Ben. I knew he would most likely be unable to travel in this weather to see me. But, I felt he had left things between us unresolved. I wondered if we were even courting anymore.

My mother tried to comfort me and tell me Ben would come as soon as the snow stopped falling and tell me that time would lessen his pain. And I could only pray she was right. I did pray about Ben and our future together. I even prayed for Dr. McCray and prayed that somehow he would find healing for whatever was ailing him. I felt it was more than my rejection of him. I truly didn't know what was wrong with the man, but I knew only God could help him. I just wanted him to stay away from me, away from Ben.

By the fourth day, the snow had stopped falling, and my father reluctantly agreed I could ride over to see Georgie at Kenrick Farms. I bundled up warmly and couldn't help but feel relieved as the white farmhouse came into view. Georgie would help me through this, she always did.

Henry and Keane were in the barn, working with the Percheron horses, and after I petted Ophelia, the foal, I made my way into the kitchen to find Georgie finishing a batch of cookies.

"Oh Val, I have been so anxious to see you and speak with you. So many things have happened," she said, hugging me and pouring us tea. I sat at the table, and she sighed, reluctant it seemed to speak about something.

"Val, Niall and Ava are getting married," she said softly.

The news did shock me a little, but it didn't hurt. "Well, I suppose I wasn't too hard to get over then, was I?" I asked with a chuckle.

She sighed. "I do not think it is his idea. I think it is forced," she said reluctantly.

I shrugged. "Well, it doesn't bother me if that is what you are worried about. I am in love with Ben, but I fear Dr. McCray and his early morning visit has ruined things for us," I confessed with tears filling my eyes. I explained to her our conversation, how I feared I had been too honest with Ben in relaying Dr. McCray's words of love and marriage, and how Ben had not returned to see me.

"It would have been wrong not to tell him, Valynn; if he should find out later, he would never have trusted you again," Georgie insisted.

"He asked me if I had feelings for Niall, and I wanted to be honest with him. I even told him that I could see the difference in the way I felt around Niall compared to him. I told him he made me feel cherished as no one has before. But now I wish I had said nothing. Oh, Georgie! I am in love with him and it hurts so terribly," I said, crying on her shoulder.

She wrapped her arms around me and let me cry. "Oh Val, we can only pray for God's will to be done," she whispered.

I nodded, knowing she was right. But it didn't lessen the ache in my chest.

Jori woke from her nap, and I snuggled her closely and cherished her sweet baby smell. Would I ever have my own babies to rock and sing to? Would they have warm brown eyes and dark brown hair? I couldn't even think of it now, it hurt too much.

Georgie and I baked a few pies, talking about my sisters and how fast my nephew Johnny and her little Jori were growing. It passed the time but did little to ease my aching heart.

Just before sunset, I headed to the barn to return home. Perhaps Ben would try and come over to see me tonight. I had just untied my mare when I heard his voice. "Valynn." I closed my eyes, knowing he wasn't truly there, but so many times he had found me in the barn and called to me. I lifted my foot in the stirrup when again I heard Dr. McCray. "Valynn, please, I need to speak with you."

I whirled around and nearly fell beneath my horse, forgetting my foot in the stirrup. "Niall McCray! When will you ever learn not to startle me?" I yelled, angry and embarrassed as he quickly helped me up.

He gave me a weak grin, not a confident one like he always had been before. This time, there was hurt hidden behind his eyes.

"What do you want?" I asked coldly.

I watched as he swallowed hard, his tormented eyes searched mine. "I need to tell you something important. I need you to understand," he said softly.

"I have already heard," I said, lifting my chin higher.

He nodded. "You haven't heard the true story, and I need to explain. Please hear me out," he pleaded.

I sighed and nodded.

"The afternoon we played cards here at Kenrick Farms and I was to have dinner with Ava that evening, I arrived and found her outside crying. She was hysterical; her father was arranging a marriage to a man she despised back East. She was a mess; her hair was half down, her gown dirty from kneeling in the grass. I had never seen her so upset. It didn't help that I had told her the last time I had dined with her that I had feelings for you and that I wanted to court you and you alone," he paused, and I looked surprised.

"It didn't go well, to say it nicely. But that night I was to dine with her family as well, and I should have cancelled but didn't. I regret that now. Anyway, I tried to calm her down, but she was going crazy, grabbing my coat, and it was as if she was out of her head. Her father came out, and of course, assumed the worst. She tried to tell her father that I had just arrived and was trying to help her, but I could see the doubt in his eyes. I suffered through dinner and once again told her my plans to court you. I thought nothing of it until she came into town and asked me to take her to the dance. I told her I planned on asking you, and she went all crazy again. She told me if I didn't take her, that she would tell her father that I had compromised her the night he had come upon us. So, I took her to the dance. She could tell that I couldn't keep my eyes off you and Ben, and on the drive home, she told me she loved me. I told her plainly that I was in love with you. I left her crying at her front door, only to be awakened an hour later, in my home, by Fredrick Stein;

he insisted I marry Ava. She told him I compromised her, and he knew he would never get her back East to marry. So, that is how my soon to be marriage has come about. It was after he left that I came here, hoping to convince you to run away with me."

I looked him in the eyes and saw he was sincere. "I am sorry for you, Niall; although, it is of your own doing. Courting several women at a time, what good can come of it?" I asked softly.

He nodded, looking completely defeated. "I just needed you to know the truth. I fear some ugly rumors are circulating, and I do not wish to hurt you anymore than I have. I am sorry for the way I came to you the other morning. Keane had every right to hit me. I was out of line. Fredrick had just left me and I was desperate. I couldn't imagine marrying anyone but you, and for a short while, I suppose, I too lost my head," he said tenderly.

I nodded. "You are forgiven," I said, wondering why I had said such a thing.

"Thank you, Valynn. I do not deserve your forgiveness. But, I pray we can somehow live our lives without hard feelings," he said softly.

"I will harbor no hard feelings for you. I wish you and Ava happiness," I said, assuring him I would do my part.

He shook his head. "I am more worried about myself, Valynn. I worry about having to watch you, and Ben. Please, do not invite me to your wedding, I could not bear it," he pleaded softly.

I swallowed hard. "I will not. Besides, we were just courting, and after finding out you came here begging me to run away with you, Ben has not returned to see me. Perhaps it has been the snow, I do not know," I said with tears filling my eyes.

Dr. McCray groaned. "I am sorry, Valynn. If I see Ben, I will apologize," he assured me.

I thanked him, and he helped me onto my horse. I looked into his green eyes, and I knew I had forgiven him. I felt there was now closure between us, and it was a great relief to me.

CHAPTER SIX

"Valynn, Georgie sent Henry over with a message asking if you could come and help her for a few hours?" Mother asked, finding me in the parlor where I worked on the mending.

"Of course! Do you need me?" I asked, excited to spend the afternoon with my sister and niece.

"No dear, go on over," she said smiling.

I put on my coat but found the day warmer than usual, and the snow finally starting to melt. Would Ben come tonight? I hadn't seen him for a week this day, and my heart ached to see his warm brown eyes. I ached to know if he still cared for me.

Henry rode back with me across the fields and took my mare as I dismounted.

I rushed into the cheery red and white kitchen, and froze in my tracks, as I saw Ben sitting with Keane and Georgie at the table. He looked so handsome sitting there, his eyes revealing his surprise that I had shown up. Then, my heart nearly stopped. If he could make it to Kenrick Farms, he could've have made it to see me.

"Ben," I said softly.

He jumped to his feet and smiled warmly. "Valynn," he whispered, his eyes drinking me in.

I blushed, embarrassed and hurt that he hadn't come to call on me.

"I need Georgie in the barn for a little while. Please listen out for Jori; she is napping in the bedroom," Keane said, rushing my sister out the back door before she had her coat on.

I hadn't even answered him.

"It is so good to see you, Valynn," Ben said softly.

I realized I still had my coat on, and I turned away from him and took it off, hanging it on the coat rack by the door. "It is good to see you, too, Ben," I said softly, not daring to look at him. I found I could not face him; I stood like an imbecile staring at the wall where the coats were hung.

"I have missed you, Valynn," he said tenderly.

I turned to find him standing close to me, and I forced myself to look into his eyes. And oh my heart! *It would never be the same.* Tears filled my eyes, and I looked down at my hands nervously. "I have missed you, too," I whispered. Why hadn't he come to see me?

Warm hands reached out for mine, and he kissed my knuckles softly, making my breath catch in my chest. "I can't stand being away from you," he whispered.

My eyes searched his, questioning.

"Mother Nature had best be done with the snow; I can't go another week like this last one," he said so tenderly.

"But, the weather, it cleared yesterday," I said as tears spilled down my cheeks, making me want to curse. I hated feeling this way, and yet I loved it all at the same time.

"I am sorry, Valynn. I had hastily tried to come and see you three days ago. My horse slipped on ice and injured her leg. She is still healing. I am only here today because Keane had driven out to see Drew, and I begged him to bring me to you. We were just warming up over coffee before heading to your house when you came," he said.

I gasped. "You were coming to see me?" I asked, surprised.

He looked puzzled but smiled.

"I assumed…I thought…I thought you changed your mind. You were so upset over Dr. McCray, and then you never returned. I knew the weather was bad, but then….," I stopped and took a breath as a sob caught in my throat. I pulled my hands away and covered my face, embarrassed. Could Ben still have feelings for me?

"Valynn, Sweetheart, do not cry," Ben said, pulling me into his warm embrace.

I had been right that first night I wondered about his embrace; it felt like heaven.

"I have been going crazy thinking about you. I was afraid you would think badly of me, the way I left things. I am so sorry, Valynn," Ben whispered into my hair.

"Ben Weston," I said, hitting my hands on his arms. I hated being an emotional mess like this. "Don't you ever do that to me again!" I threatened.

Ben laid his head against mine, and I found he was quickly forgiven. "Please don't be angry with me,

Valynn. I missed you so. I have been in the worst torment," he whispered.

I clung to him, and he held me even tighter. "I have regretted telling you about him. I always say the wrong things. I should have just kept quiet. You should know, it is my worst downfall," I whispered.

Ben kissed the top of my head tenderly. "I love your honesty, Valynn. I was hurt, but I needed to know what he had done. It was not your fault. I was mainly jealous and wanted to beat the daylights out him. It was probably a good thing I was snowed in. It gave me time to cool my temper towards Dr. McCray," Ben chuckled.

"You have nothing to be jealous of, Ben," I whispered. I was in love, and being in Ben's arms was worth all the suffering of the last week.

Ben lifted my head tenderly from his chest, his brown eyes sparkling. "I love you, Valynn Andley," he whispered with a smile.

My heart raced at his confession. Ben still loved me! I smiled warmly. "I love *you*, Ben Weston," I said, breathless from his nearness and sweetness.

Ben smiled, surprised at my confession. "I have prayed for so long to hear those words from your sweet lips," he whispered to me.

My heart raced.

"I know it is forward of me, but might I kiss you, Valynn?" he asked nervously.

I blushed and nodded.

His warm lips pressed against mine softly at first, and then he pulled me closer. His kiss intensified, sending every silly thought I had straight out the window. He finally broke the kiss. Breathlessly he hugged me close to him. "I pray you do not want a long courtship," he teased.

I smiled and hugged him tightly. I prayed he did not as well. I knew, without a doubt, I wanted nothing more than to be his wife. But I wanted him to be certain of his feelings and, I wanted to be asked properly, so I remained quiet and hopeful.

Georgie and Keane came back into the house, and we played a hand of cards, and of course, I won.

Ben shook his head as Keane once again went into his competitive rant about how I had to be cheating. I laughed so hard I could hardly breathe. After winning my third hand of cards, Ben was rubbing his head in frustration. "This just isn't right," Ben said, shaking his head and smiling at me.

"You and Keane are just sore losers," I said, laughing.

Ben smiled. "Oh, do not worry, Valynn; I will get you back for that," Ben teased.

I laughed. "Well, I hope it is not by playing cards, for we all can see how well that is working for you," I teased back.

Ben's face turned red, and he smiled mischievously. "No! Not with playing cards. Spring is coming; I reckon I can find me a mess of tree frogs," he threatened.

My smile quickly faded, and I raised an eyebrow- just the word frog terrified me.

Everyone burst into laughter, except for me. Ben knew he had me and gloated the rest of the afternoon. But I loved every minute of it.

It was time for me to return home, and Ben walked me out to the barn to get my horse. We held hands, and I sensed he didn't want the afternoon to end any more than I did. "I wish I had a way to take you home," he whispered.

I smiled. "Henry will ride with me. It is getting late, and Weston farms is nearly five miles from here," I reminded.

He sighed and nodded.

"I had fun," I whispered, blushing as he pulled me closely.

"Oh, Valynn, you are always fun. I wish I could spend every minute of every day with you," he said, hugging me to his chest.

I hugged him in return. "I know," I whispered.

He leaned back surprised. "You do? You feel the same way?" he asked, smiling tenderly.

I nodded. His lips found mine, and I kissed him with all the love I held in my heart. "Valynn, Sweetheart, you are making this difficult for me," Ben said, breaking the kiss.

I blushed at how boldly I had been returning his kiss.

"Can I see you tomorrow evening if I can borrow a horse from Drew?" Ben asked softly.

"You had best come, or else!" I teased.

He smiled. "Or else what?" he asked, nearly to kiss me again.

Every sassy thought flew straight out of my head, and I kissed him once more.

Ben sighed and shook his head, hating to part from me. "Have a good evening, Valynn," he said after helping me onto my horse.

I wished Ben a goodnight, waited for Henry, and then rode home with my head and heart in the clouds. My lips still tingled from Ben's kisses, and I had to thank God for creating such a marvelous man, even if he did like frogs.

The next day seemed to drag by as I waited for evening and for Ben's promised visit. I rushed through my chores and bathed, washing my hair and carefully wrapping the long strands in rag curlers. I chose a dark blue calico dress with a square collar, and Genevieve carefully arranged my hair for me high on my head and leaving a few strands of curls down one shoulder.

"So Val, why is it you are courting Ben Weston now, and not Dr. McCray?" my youngest sister Augusta asked me softly as I finished dressing.

I sighed and sat on the bed, pulling her close. Augusta had always been our little baby doll. "I know it must seem confusing for you, Gusta, but when you're choosing to allow a man to court you, there are important things to consider. Ben Weston surprised me, completely surprised me, by having those things that are important to me," I said, smiling as my stomach fluttered at the thought of Ben's kisses the day before.

"But didn't you like Dr. McCray? He seemed to like you very much when he came to take you for the sleigh ride?" she asked, confused.

I brushed her hair back from her sweet face. "In the beginning, I did like Dr. McCray, very much. I found him to be quite handsome. But his actions toward me confused me and made me uncertain. You see, he also likes Ava Stein. In fact, they will marry this Sunday," I said tenderly. But the thought did not hurt me. "Even though a man is handsome, it doesn't mean he is good or that he will make a good husband. You have to pray and truly look for those important qualities. When I did, Niall McCray just didn't have them," I said honestly.

She nodded as if she understood now. "But Ben Weston does, I am glad," she said, smiling.

I smiled and hugged her tightly.

"I am as well. Ben Weston is much more handsome than Isaac Stein or Niall McCray," Genevieve said, smiling wistfully.

I sighed contentedly. It seemed forever ago that I courted Isaac, and yet it had only been a few months. I had courted Isaac for a year and never once felt for him the way I felt for Ben Weston. I was suddenly so thankful Isaac had left to find gold.

I heard a knock at the door downstairs and then my father greeting Ben.

"He is here. How do I look?" I asked anxiously.

Both my sisters smiled and assured me I looked fine.

I tried to calmly walk downstairs and not seem too eager, but when my eyes met Ben's, my feet sped up as I reached for his hand.

His eyes searched my face, and I blushed as I wondered if he was thinking of our kisses the day before? I had thought of little else. His blush seemed to say he had. "You look beautiful, Valynn."

I blushed as I thanked him. "I hope you like roast beef," I said, taking his coat and hanging it on the hook for guests.

He nodded with a smile.

I knew he ate with his brother Drew and my friend Millie often, but I suddenly wanted to take care of this man before me. I wanted to see to his meals and laundry and sit on the back porch and watch the stars with him and Yonder. I took his arm and led him into the dining room.

"Welcome, Ben!" my mother greeted.

He nodded and greeted her and my two sisters.

"We are excited to hear you and Valynn will be seeing more of one another," she said, smiling.

Ben blushed and looked to me; his eyes told me he was happy as well. I squeezed his arm tenderly.

We all sat down and held hands as my father said the blessing over the meal. I had to smile as my sisters watched Ben curiously, even wistfully. He was terribly handsome, and *he was mine*. I felt so full of pride that I could bust.

"Valynn made the potatoes, Ben," my mother bragged.

I blushed and tried to shush her.

Ben smiled and nodded. "They are quite good, Valynn," he said, winking. He knew just what my sweet little mother was up to. My father watched us pleased.

"How big is your house, Ben?"

I gasped and looked at Augusta. Genevieve kicked her under the table.

Ben smiled as my mother looked horrified. "Well, it isn't too big, but not too small. There is a kitchen, a dining room, a washroom, and parlor, oh, and three bedrooms."

I smiled, for it sounded perfect to me. I loved farmhouses.

"We have five bedrooms here. Three isn't very many if you have babies."

I dropped my fork in utter shock and humiliation as I stared at my youngest sister. I was still staring at her when I leaned over and bumped heads with Ben as he bent over to pick it up for me. We both laughed as we held our throbbing heads, our cheeks flushed.

"You have a hard head, Ben Weston!" I teased.

He smiled mischievously. "Perhaps it is you that has the hard head," he said, baiting me. I laughed, for he was most likely right.

"She..," my little sister began.

But thankfully my mother interrupted her. "Augusta, you may be quiet now," my mother said sweetly, giving my sister 'the eye.' *I had never been so relieved.*

After dinner we retired to the parlor. I was thankful my mother sent my sisters upstairs for the evening. There would be no more talk of babies and numbers of bedrooms this night. Although I longed to be a mother one day, I wasn't ready to discuss such things just yet.

The fire roared nicely in the fireplace as I sat on the sofa, anxious for time alone to talk with Ben. "So, I heard Niall and Ava are marrying Sunday," he said.

I frowned, for I didn't want to talk about Niall McCray. I nodded. "So I have heard."

Ben nodded again.

"How was your..," but he interrupted me.

"I have to ask, Valynn, how did you hear the news?"

I frowned. Why was he asking me about this now? I had missed him terribly. I didn't want to talk about Niall and

Ava. "I learned the day before I saw you at Kenrick Farms, after the snow. Georgie told me first, and then Niall was in the barn when I was leaving. He wanted to tell me himself and apologize for his actions the night of the dance." I watched as Ben's handsome jaw tensed, and he stiffened. I laid my hand on his arm tenderly. What had I said wrong?

He nodded.

"Ben, what is it?" I asked, concerned.

He sighed. "It just seems as if you two keep getting thrown together somehow."

I sighed and smiled. "Ben Weston! Are you jealous? You truly have no reason to be," I said tenderly.

But Ben shook his head. "He is in love with you, Valynn. He kissed you before I did. Is that not supposed to bother me when I hear you two were in the barn talking?" His brown eyes searched mine intensely.

I didn't like this conversation. Not at all! "Ben, I was leaving! He had just arrived. He simply wanted to tell me he was marrying Ava before the ugly rumors started. He had it in his head at the dance that somehow I cared for him. I set him straight. He even apologized for causing trouble between us," I said.

Ben frowned. "What trouble?" he asked.

I sighed. *I should not have said that.* It was my life story. "I thought you were angry with me. You hadn't come to see me, and you had been upset about Niall coming to Kenrick farms and trying to convince me to run away with him. I told him that it upset you, and I hadn't seen

125

you. He apologized for any trouble he caused. It was nothing more than that. Why are you acting this way?" I asked, getting as angry as he was.

"You discussed *us*, with him? He looks at you like he could eat you up, Valynn! I don't think he has honorable thoughts toward you at all! It makes me so mad; I could knock the daylights out of him. Can't you see, Valynn? I am in love with you. So much it hurts me, something terrible. I can't stand the thoughts of you even talking to him," Ben said angrily.

I gasped. "I didn't seek him out, Ben! He was in the barn when I was leaving. He wanted to apologize; he said he wanted no hard feelings between us. *I* didn't do anything wrong!" I said defensively. I felt panicked. I loved Ben- why couldn't he see it.

Ben bowed his head, but he was still quite upset. I could only wonder what had caused this when just minutes ago, he was happy.

"I am in love with *you*, Ben," I whispered, taking his hand in mine.

He stood quickly, ready to bolt.

I jumped to my feet and stomped my foot as hard as I could. "Ben Weston, you are acting like a twelve year old boy again!" I said with my temper flaring.

His handsome jaw tensed until I was certain he would have no teeth left. "I will bid you a goodnight then, Valynn," he said, rushing to the door.

"Ben, come back here and fight this out with me!" I yelled. What on earth had happened to cause this fight anyway?

He turned at the door and looked at me with a look of regret. And then he left. He didn't come back, apologizing for over reacting.

I paced the parlor for nearly two hours, praying that he would. He had even forgotten his hat.

Finally, in defeat, I lay in my bed, weeping and trying to understand what had gone wrong, worrying over his handsome head getting too cold in the night air without his hat. Blasted-man!

I walked the house numbly as I did my chores on Saturday. I had expected Ben to be waiting at my door at daylight. But he wasn't.

I sat at the table with my parents, telling them what had happened, relaying to them my confusion. They both shook their heads, agreeing that the encounter with Niall in the barn had not been my fault and agreeing that it sounded quite innocent. Tomorrow, Ava and Niall would marry; perhaps then Ben would see that it was over. I wanted nothing to do with Niall, and he was marrying Ava. I had tried my best to tell him so, but he was nearly accusing me of lying.

I had no idea what to do with this heartache; I hurt so badly, I was certain I might die. And it only served to fuel my temper even more. I was innocent! I didn't deserve this treatment! *Ben Weston was still a pain in the backside!*

That afternoon I rode over to Kenrick Farms, looking for Georgie. Perhaps she could help me to understand Ben. My brother-in-law, Keane, had given her some hard times early in their marriage. But they seemed to have worked through them somehow. I sighed; Georgie was a saint compared to me. I lacked the patience to let Ben work through his jealously. And I was determined that was all this was, pure jealousy! I hadn't done anything to make him jealous, and he was treating me terribly because of it.

I walked into the kitchen quietly and smiled weakly as I saw my sister rocking Jori in the parlor. My heart ached at the tender sight. Would I ever know such motherly bliss? The way things were going with my love life, I was beginning to doubt it. Isaac found gold more interesting than me. I hadn't been enough to completely captivate Niall McCray and now Ben. Tears filled my eyes. Ben was the only one I cared about. And my heart ached as I had never experienced before, and I hated it.

Georgie smiled and stood, laying her sleeping baby in the basinet, and then rushed to hug me.

I followed her back into the kitchen, and she poured us tea. "What is wrong, Valynn?" she asked, concerned.

I felt my tears, and I hated crying. I wasn't an overly emotional female as a few of my sisters were. I had always been strong, resilient, until now.

"Ben and I had a fight. And I do not even know what about," I said, breaking down.

She smiled tenderly and hugged me to her. "It is normal to have a spat now and then," she whispered.

I shook my head no. "Ben was acting as if Niall and I had done something wrong the day Niall told me of his approaching marriage. Somehow Ben found out Niall was here, and that we had talked. He wouldn't listen to a word I said. He was so angry and jealous. He left me! He walked right out! And he hasn't returned to say he was sorry." I lay my head on the kitchen table, and Georgie rubbed my head just as she had when I was a little girl.

"Oh Val, men are such peculiar creatures. Keane used to get jealous of Dr. Anderson, remember?"

I lifted my head and wiped my eyes, nodding. I did remember.

"When you're newly in love, for man at least, I think there is a very strong urge to protect the woman they love. Almost territorial, like animals," she giggled.

I frowned. "But Isaac never acted this way," I said, confused.

"But Niall has, and now Ben. Perhaps you were right; perhaps you and Isaac were more friends than in love. I think perhaps that Ben is so crazy in love with you that he jumped to conclusions and that it is his fear of losing you once again that is making him act like this," she offered.

I sighed. "He is being ridiculous! I knew he was a pain in the backside," I complained, but I loved him dearly.

Georgie giggled and smoothed my hair back from my wet cheeks.

Suddenly, the kitchen door opened and Keane came in smiling. "Look what I found wandering around on foot," he said.

He moved out of the way, and there stood Ben. His eyes lit up like the morning sun when he saw me. I wanted to run to him, beg him to stop being so ridiculous, but my pride kept me from moving.

"Valynn!" he said with what looked like hope in his eyes.

"Keane, could you come with me... outside?" Georgie asked, moving toward the kitchen door. Keane gave me a wink and followed my sister outside.

I stood nervously. I was still very angry with Ben. What was he doing wandering around out in the countryside and on foot?

He moved toward me a few steps and stopped, twirling his hat in his hands nervously. "Valynn, I was on my way to see you. I have been the biggest fool...," he stopped and swallowed hard.

My heart raced, but I stayed quiet. Ben was a shy man, but he needed to learn to share his feelings with me. And I needed to learn not to rush him. His eyes pleaded with mine, but he needed to apologize a little better than that.

"Drew is gone with the horse, so I left this morning after chores were done. I had to see you. I need to beg for your forgiveness," he said, taking another step. Again his eyes pleaded for help.

I lifted my chin higher. I hadn't done anything wrong; I wanted to hear him say so.

"You have been crying," he said, concerned.

I sighed. It was all I could do not to just forgive him and run into those strong arms of his. "You were going to apologize," I said rather impatiently.

Ben sighed. "Valynn, I am sorry. I lost control of my temper. I was terribly jealous. You didn't deserve that," he said tenderly.

I felt a fresh wave of tears. He was doing a good job of melting my reserve. He took another step closer, hesitantly. Somehow I could see in those beautiful brown eyes, he was wagering on whether to hold me or not, if I would forgive him or not. I took one step closer, pushing down my raging pride. He was more important to me than being right.

"I am not in love with Niall, Ben. If I was, I would have acted on it. I am not one to play games," I said softly.

His eyes showed me his sincere relief and he nodded. "I have always liked that about you, Valynn, your directness," he admitted shyly.

I sighed. "Then why on earth didn't you believe me then? Ben Weston, you broke my heart leaving like you did," I said, fighting down my stubborn pride and once again trying to rush him to hold me. I was hopeless and would never change, I was certain.

"Valynn, you've got me so tail side up in love with you, Sweetheart, I don't even know what is wrong with me," he gushed.

And there I went, running right into his arms. His kisses were warm and wonderful. They mingled with my tears, and I clung to him as he whispered his love for me. And whispered how sorry he was for making me cry.

"You're such a pain in the backside, Ben Weston," I wept.

He sighed and kissed me again, making me forget the near two days my heart had hung in suspense. "Forgive me, Sweetheart, please," he whispered.

I nodded, and he hugged me close.

"I love you, Valynn Andley. And I will never doubt your love for me again," he promised.

I hugged him even tighter. "You had best not, for I might not be so nice next time. I have a temper if you have forgotten so soon," I warned.

He chuckled warmly. "You're awfully cute when you stomp your tiny feet," he whispered.

I slapped his arm, hard, and he winced and kissed me before I could get angry. I pulled back, breathless, and smiled. "Best not kiss me like that again, Ben Weston."

His brown eyes twinkled, and I found I could spend the rest of my life, every day, staring into them. "And why not?" he whispered.

I smiled and blushed. "You wouldn't be able to get rid of me, should you decide you wanted to," I said, feeling shy now, but knowing, we had kissed enough for a few weeks at least.

"I never wish to get rid of you, Sweetheart. You forget, I have prayed and fasted for this, and I nearly blew it. I won't be so foolish again," he whispered tenderly.

I lay my head on his chest. "I love you, Ben! Even if you are a pain, you are my pain," I whispered. It shouldn't be permissible to love someone so much, to hurt so much, but I did. And it was a little more than frightening.

Sunday came, and I begged Father and Mother to allow me to miss church and stay at home. Ava and Dr. McCray would be married today, and the celebration would last all afternoon and into the evening. Ava was the only daughter of the wealthy Stein family, and I knew it would be quite a celebration. I liked Ava and wished her no ill, but I felt it would be awkward to attend given the circumstances. They finally agreed with me, and I was left alone for the day.

I bathed and washed my hair, read part of a book, but I had to admit, I was lonely and restless. I wasn't one who liked to be alone often; growing up with four sisters, I was used to noise and cherished it.

I decided to work on my wedding ring quilt and was quite ashamed I had never finished it while I courted Isaac. Every young woman I knew had made her wedding ring quilt years in advance, except for me. Even my sister Genevieve, at sixteen, had more done on her quilt than I had.

I sat before the fire letting my hair dry as I sewed the tiny scraps of dark blue, light blue, a soft pink floral, and a blue and white floral material together, forming the rings. My heart skipped a beat as I thought of laying this quilt out over my marriage bed someday. I prayed it would be in Ben's and my home. Had Ben gone to the wedding today? Would he stay for the dancing? I didn't know what Ben would do, for we hadn't remembered to talk about it after making up the day before. I wished he could spend the evening with me, but without a chaperone, it wouldn't be proper.

I quickly gave up sewing, realizing I wasn't going to achieve much this day, and so I baked. I baked a chocolate cake and then made cinnamon rolls.

After cleaning up the kitchen, I heard a knock at the door. Surely Ben knew it wasn't proper to come alone. I peeked out the parlor window and froze. It was Isaac Stein. I groaned. I had enough of men all ready- why wasn't he in the hills searching for gold?

I opened the door just a crack. My dry hair still hung to my waist, and I wore an old work dress, not to mention, I was alone. "Isaac, why aren't you at your sister's celebration?" I asked rather bluntly.

He grinned, his grey eyes just the same as the day he left. "I saw you were not with your family, and your mother said you were unwell. I just got back into town last night for Ava's wedding. I had to see you," he said cautiously.

"Well, I cannot invite you in," I said, wishing him to leave.

"Could you sit on the front porch with me, Valynn? I just wanted to know if it's true...about.....you and Ben?" he asked, looking a little hurt.

I sighed and joined him on the front porch.

"You look as beautiful as ever, Valynn," he complimented.

But I felt nothing for Isaac, except a fond friendship. We had been good friends since we were children, and although we had courted, the romantic feelings had never sparked between us- at least for me they hadn't.

"I saw Ben at church this morning. He was acting strange, and I had to nearly wrestle it out of him. He said you two were courting," Isaac said, searching my face for answers.

I nodded and smiled. "Yes, we are. I am very happy, Isaac," I said, letting Isaac know right off that I didn't wish to go back to courting him.

"You couldn't wait for me, huh?" he asked playfully, but I heard the hurt underlined in his words.

"No, I couldn't. I told you I wouldn't wait before you left. I didn't pursue Ben, but I do feel it is God's will. It all happened so quickly, but I am in love with Ben," I said, being honest.

Isaac playfully grabbed his heart as if I had wounded him, and I had to smile. "Don't sugar coat it or anything, Valynn," he laughed. I shrugged; he knew me well. "Well, I guess Ben is about the only man I would back down for," Isaac said, standing to leave.

I thanked him for being understanding.

He shrugged. "I heard I wasn't the only heart you broke while I was gone," he said in reference to Dr. McCray.

I felt my cheeks growing red and I clenched my fists tight. "Isaac Stein, you left me to find gold! And if you are referring to Dr. McCray, it is all his own doing. He could not discern his own heart!" I stomped my foot hard on the wooden porch.

Isaac smiled, holding his hands up to protect himself and backing away a few steps. "I was just repeating what I had heard, Valynn. No need in getting all riled up," he laughed.

I shook my head. "Perhaps you had best not believe everything you hear then," I said, trying to calm down. Why were men so infuriating?

Isaac nodded. "Perhaps you are right, I will try not to," he said tenderly. His eyes searched my face, and I had to look away. He wasn't truly in love with me; he just thought he was.

"It wasn't God's will for us, Isaac. Nor for Niall and me. God has saved Ben for me. And I love him, I truly do," I admitted, not wanting to hurt Isaac but to force him to see the facts and get over me.

"I wish you love and happiness, Valynn. Ben is my friend, and you have my blessing, not that you wanted it or anything," he said tenderly.

I smiled and wiped away a tear that appeared out of nowhere. I had never been a crier. Was this what happened when you fell in love? I didn't care for this part of it.

"Thank you, Isaac. It does make me happy to know you and Ben will still be friends," I admitted.

He smiled one last smile and then rode away. I was greatly relieved and locked the front door, determined not to answer it if another male came calling today unless, perhaps, Ben came. I smiled, *only for Ben*.

Chapter Seven

But Ben did not come that evening, and after my parents and younger sisters came home late, we sat at the dining room table as they told me of Dr. McCray's wedding.

I told them several times I didn't want to hear about it. But Augusta went on and on about the elaborate food table, the Italian ices, and the large bouquets of roses the Steins had shipped in.

Genevieve talked of the dancing and of how Ben stood next to her, questioning her all evening if I was truly all right. "He never danced, not one dance. He was beside himself without you there," she giggled.

It did make me feel a little better that he had been miserable without me. But why hadn't he come to see me?

Father ordered the younger girls up to bed, and then he patted my hand, wanting me to stay with him at the table. "It was a solemn wedding, my Val," my father said quietly.

I sighed. That didn't make me feel any better.

"Ava looked pleased, but poor Dr. McCray! I do not know if I have ever seen such a tormented man," Mother said.

"I am proud of you, Valynn, for your praying heart, for your discernment and wisdom. It seems Niall compromised Ava, and I can't help but think that could have been you," Father said emotionally.

"She tricked him into it," I said softly. "He found me at Kenrick Farms. He wanted to explain what happened. But, he allowed her to do so. It was the wrong choices he made that put him in such a position," I said, hugging my father's shoulders. "I do hope God can help him to heal and that they can work things out between them," I said, meaning every word.

Mother and Father agreed and kissed me goodnight.

I went to bed with a heavy heart for Dr. McCray and Ava. I couldn't help but wonder that if I married Ben, would he prove to be a happy groom. I remembered my sister Celia's wedding and Georgie's as well, for they were on the same day. John had looked so happy when he held Celia's hands. But poor Keane had looked like he was facing a death sentence. But God had worked things out between Georgie and Keane, and now there was no denying Keane loved my sister with all that he had. Perhaps soon Dr. McCray could feel that way about Ava as well. I fell asleep praying it would be so.

The evening after Dr. McCray's wedding, Ben came by after supper. I was afraid he wouldn't come. It was getting rather late, and I felt my eyes widen with surprise as my father showed him into the parlor.

"Ben!" I squealed and rushed to him, my heart racing.

His smile lit up the dimness of the room as he took my hands in his.

After my family left us alone and retired to the dining room, I sat next to Ben on the sofa.

"I was worried about you, Valynn. Your mother said you were unwell, but Genevieve said you were just fine. Why didn't you come to the wedding?" Ben asked softly. He looked concerned, perhaps thinking I still felt something for Dr. McCray. But he had promised me he wouldn't doubt my love for him again. Could men truly not remember their own promises?

"Ben Weston, if you even start thinking it was because I hold feelings for Niall McCray, I will tan your hide good!" I said with my temper surfacing. I sighed heavily, trying to calm myself down.

Ben's eyes searched mine, as if he were thinking carefully through his next words. I silently admonished him to do so. "I was just surprised and disappointed you hadn't come, that is all," he said, lifting my chin to look into my eyes.

He quickly kissed me, trying to make me forget we were nearly arguing again. And it worked, *quite nicely*.

"I didn't feel it right that I attend. It isn't because their marrying bothered me, it doesn't. I wish them happiness, truly. But I like Ava; I know that she knows about Niall's infatuation with me. I didn't want things to be awkward, and I felt that it would have been," I said, brushing his hair from his forehead.

He smiled tenderly, looking so much like the boy I knew as a child. "You like to act tough, but you have a soft heart, Valynn Andley. I love that about you- sass and sweetness, wrapped in pure beauty!"

140

I smiled at his tender words.

"Isaac has returned," he said, sighing.

I stiffened. *Here we went again*. I nodded that I was aware of his return.

He looked surprised.

I covered my head with my hands and groaned.

"Why are you doing that?" Ben asked, lifting my head from my hands.

I sighed. "Because I don't want to argue with you, I don't want you to be jealous and leave again," I said, feeling quite defeated. Why hadn't anyone warned me love was so difficult? I would surely have sworn off men if I had known.

"I promise to try my best, not to be jealous," he said tenderly.

I frowned. "Isaac came by, right in the middle of the wedding celebration," I admitted.

Ben sighed and nodded. "We all wondered where he had run off to. I should have suspected he would have come here."

I rubbed his arm tenderly, trying to reassure him of my affection for him. "He came to hear it from me that we were courting. He said that you had confessed it at church... after a great deal of wrestling it out of you," I said, smiling.

Ben blushed and nodded, "I didn't want to hurt him, and yet, I wanted him to stay far away from you. And what does he do, he runs right over here." Ben shook his head, working through his frustration.

I took his hand and entwined our fingers together. He rewarded me with a gentle smile. "Well, I told him that I was in love with you. And that it hadn't been God's will for him and me. I was painfully blunt, I fear, but he wished us happiness. He assured me that you and he were still friends. He will get over me soon, I promise," I whispered.

Ben sighed. "I feel like I have to fight off every male in Crawford. I don't like being jealous. It isn't really like me; at least, I didn't think it was. I just love you so much, Valynn. I feel like every day that we are courting is just another day I could lose you. I don't deserve you, Valynn," he whispered.

I lay my head against his shoulder, sniffing and smiling at his clean laundered smell; it was wonderful. "But *you* hold my heart, Ben Weston! I don't want anyone else, only you. I couldn't find a better man than you. You're a good man, a Godly man, who has prayed for me for a year without me even knowing. You help your neighbors, you work hard. It is I who doesn't deserve you. You are much too good for me. And... I am afraid, after those kisses at Kenrick Farms, you'll never get rid of me now," I giggled.

Ben hugged me closely, and I felt like everything was right in the world when he held me. "Valynn, I do love you. I will fight off however many beaus that come along, one frog at a time," he teased.

I had to laugh thinking of Ben, now a grown man, throwing frogs, especially at Dr. McCray and Isaac.

"You know, spring plowing and planting are just a month away. It is such a busy time. I will hardly see you for weeks at a time," he said tenderly.

I squeezed his hand in mine and sighed. "Shh....do not remind me," I whispered. "You do not really need wheat and corn this year, do you?" I asked teasingly, looking up into his eyes.

To my surprise, he kissed me. "I need you, Valynn," he whispered, pressing his forehead gently to mine and causing my breath to catch in my chest.

My stomach fluttered. I wanted to cry with happiness. I loved this man so much.

Suddenly he slid down before me on one knee. "I cannot pretend that I am all right going weeks without seeing you. I cannot hide my jealousy that you are so highly sought after. I need you, Valynn. I need you to be the first thing I see each morning, and the last thing I hold at night. I have prayed so hard for this. I know it is too soon, *but gosh-darn-it Valynn, I cannot wait any longer.* Marry me, please!" he pleaded, his brown eyes full of hope and love, a love for me alone.

I nodded with a huge grin and squealed with delight as I threw my arms around his neck and kissed him breathlessly.

"Is that a yes?" he whispered into my hair.

"Yes! Ben Weston, I will marry you," I assured him. I would truly elope with him this moment if he asked me to. I didn't want to spend another day away from him.

"Let's go tell your parents. I have already spoken to your father, but let's tell them together," Ben said, kissing my hand as I stood.

I breathed in deeply as I looked into his eyes; it meant so much to me that Ben sought my father's approval.

Ben put his arm around my shoulders as we walked toward the dining room. "Valynn, do you think you could marry me before the spring planting? I just can't bear to think of being away from you that long," Ben asked softly and anxiously.

He was so handsome and melting my heart more and more by the second. "Pick a date, Ben. I promise to be ready," I said, smiling.

"Tomorrow!" he said, teasing and kissing my forehead, but little did he know I would have readily agreed. He led me into the dining room, and with one look on my parents' faces, I knew they suspected something.

"Mr. and Mrs. Andley, I have asked Valynn to become my wife, and she has graciously agreed," Ben said nervously.

Both of my parents smiled brightly and hugged Ben and then myself, giving us their blessing and sharing in our joy.

Genevieve and Augusta were ecstatic, and I found myself dizzy with happiness as we sat down at the table with my parents and began to plan.

"I asked Valynn if she would marry before spring planting," Ben said, blushing.

I could only smile. I was not a bit embarrassed that he couldn't wait to marry me. I felt the same way.

My mother gasped, and my father laughed warmly. "But that is only a month away," my mother exclaimed.

I nodded with a smile.

She sighed and smiled, shaking her head. "You have always been my challenging one, Valynn!" she said, trying to scold me.

But it wasn't going to work. I didn't want a fancy wedding; I truly didn't care if we had a wedding at all. I would stand before Pastor Crawley tomorrow if she would let me. Somehow, I knew she wouldn't.

"How about Sunday," Ben suggested.

My mother nearly had a fit. I had to laugh. Eloping sounded better by the minute. "How about three weeks from Sunday," she retorted.

Ben was trying to be patient, but I found I couldn't be. "How about two weeks from Sunday?" I bargained.

She sighed and shook her head. "Two weeks, Valynn? You are just like Georgie and Celia. Don't you want that fancy wedding you planned as a girl? We cannot possibly pull something together so quickly," she argued.

"We can wait, Valynn, if you want your dream wedding," Ben said tenderly.

I smiled and shook my head as I looked into his eyes. "Two weeks, and it is nearly too long I fear. I don't want a fancy wedding. I just want you, Ben Weston. Dressed up and in front of our families," I whispered.

My mother sighed in defeat as my sisters both talked at once, offering us their help and suggestions. But I couldn't take my eyes off this man beside me. God couldn't have given me a better man than Ben, I knew it for certain.

By the time Ben left, it was settled. We would wed in two weeks, which would give us two full weeks of marital bliss before the plowing was to start at Weston Farms.

I could not stop smiling when I went to bed; in two weeks, I would be Mrs. Benjamin Weston. *Valynn Clarice Weston*, I cherished the sound of it and whispered it to myself at least a hundred times before I fell asleep.

I rode over to Kenrick Farms the next morning to tell Georgie our news. I found her and Mormor in the kitchen with Jori, and I squealed excitedly, scaring them both and making Jori cry.

"Valynn, how many times have I told you not to do that?" Georgie said, scolding me.

I took Jori from Mormor and began bouncing her and kissing her sweet chubby cheeks to calm her. "I am sorry, but I cannot begin to help it. I am overcome with happiness!" I said, smiling.

Georgie paused in her baking and looked hopeful.

"Ben asked me to marry him!" I said, bouncing with joy.

Georgie squealed and Mormor quickly took the baby into the parlor so we could talk without scaring her.

"Tell me everything," Georgie insisted as we set down with a cup of tea.

I told her all the sweet things Ben had said and how he had proposed. Georgie's eyes filled with tears, and I suddenly felt guilty, for she had not had it easy when she first married Keane.

"I am sorry, I am being selfish," I said, hugging her.

"No, no, these are tears of joy, silly. I am just so happy for you and Ben. You made a wise choice, Valynn," Georgie said, hugging me. I told her we wanted to marry in two weeks, and she gasped.

"We must hurry and plan, we must get Celia," she said, rushing to get a piece of stationary and a pencil.

My sister Celia was the best at throwing parties.

"What sort of cake do you want?" she asked, poised with her pencil.

I shrugged and smiled. "I just want to marry Ben! You pick for me," I said.

She sighed and shook her head. "What is Ben's favorite flavor?" she asked.

I shrugged. "I do not even know," I confessed.

She looked shocked.

"Is that bad, that I don't know?" I asked.

She shrugged. "Val, do you and Ben think you're rushing it just a little?" she asked concerned.

My heart froze in fear. I loved Georgie. I wanted her blessing. "Isn't there time to learn these things after we marry?" I didn't want to wait. I would find out this day what kind of cake he liked.

Georgie smiled. "I suppose, Val. But there are a great many things you learn *after* you marry. Sometimes things that.....oh, never mind! You are determined, and when you get something into your head, there is no changing you mind! I know you too well!" she said, sighing and patting my hand tenderly.

I tried to smile and listen to her questions. But now I was worried. Would everyone feel we were rushing? Did I care what others thought?

Just then Keane walked in, and I gasped when I saw Ben coming in behind him. "Ben," I said, rushing to him surprised.

Ben looked worried or angry, I couldn't tell which.

"What is it? What is wrong?" I asked, suddenly concerned.

"Pastor Crawley cannot perform the wedding in two weeks. He is going out of town for his mother's birthday. He will not be back until the Sunday of planting," he said, disappointed.

My heart nearly froze in fear. Was this God's way of slowing us down. Was it wrong to marry so quickly if we had both prayed and both felt it was his will?

"Oh no! Oh, Val, I am sorry for you both," Georgie said, seeing our disappointment.

I sighed and tried to smile the best I could. "Well, we can still marry in early June once the planting is finished," I said, trying to cheer Ben up, but my heart was breaking as much as his.

He pulled me to his side and hugged me. Tears filled my eyes, and I couldn't help but cry. June was four months away. It might as well be four years. "Don't cry, Sweetheart," Ben whispered into my hair.

"You know, there is another way," Keane said, speaking up.

Ben turned to look at my brother-in-law who stood smiling from ear to ear. "How is that?" Ben asked, curious, perhaps hopeful.

"You could marry this Sunday, and have the reception here at Kenrick Farms; I didn't build that fancy dance floor in my barn for nothing," he said, giving us a wink.

I gasped and looked at Ben. His eyes searched mine. "Ben, what kind of cake do you like?" I asked, still crying.

He looked at me confused.

"We will just step into the parlor," Georgie said, understanding and taking her husband by the arm.

"What are you asking, Valynn?"

Ben was terribly cute when he was confused. "I don't even know what kind of cake you like. I don't know what your favorite food is. Your favorite color," I said with my heart aching. It would kill me to postpone the wedding four months.

"Valynn, what do those things matter? You will have the rest of our lives to find out. Are you having second thoughts?" he asked.

His handsome face held his fear, and I shook my head no. I knew I loved him, and I knew I would wait no matter how long it took to marry him. "No. I just worry, are we rushing too fast?" I asked.

Ben sighed in frustration. "Valynn, I pray not. But I cannot wait any longer, Sweetheart. You consume my every thought. I can't even do my choring without messing something up, my thoughts are continually on you. I tried to milk Jasper," he admitted softly.

I smiled and let him pull me close. Then I had to laugh, for Jasper was his horse.

"You are the most important thing to me, Valynn. If you need time, I will give it to you. I have prayed for a year, and I am confident in my love, and in God's plan. But I don't want to rush you," he whispered. He pressed his forehead to mine.

I wrapped my arms around him, and he hugged me closely. I looked into his eyes and smiled. "Ben, I am challenging, and it may cause you grief. But I cannot wait four months to marry you!" I sighed.

Ben smiled. "Keane! Get that barn ready! I'm riding over to Pastor Crawley's to see if he is willing to marry us this Sunday!" he called out excitedly.

I squealed with joy as he swung me around.

Keane and Georgie smiled in the doorway.

"Don't leave, Valynn. I will hurry back," he pleaded.

I smiled. "I'm not going anywhere, Ben Weston! Now go! We only have four days! Get going," I urged, nearly pushing him out the kitchen door.

He stole a kiss, and I waved as he turned to look back at me from the yard.

I crossed my fingers and closed my eyes and prayed that God would let us marry this Sunday. June was forever away. *And I hadn't been born a patient girl.*

An hour later, Ben flew into the kitchen at Kenrick Farms. "He will do it, we can marry! Drew and Millie want to help. Keane, I will do all I can to help you ready the barn," Ben said, smiling from ear to ear.

Georgie gasped. "We must hurry and spread the word, and Valynn, we must start baking. Oh mercy! You haven't told Mother and Father yet! We need Celia!" she said, growing nervous and frazzled.

I laughed and hugged Ben tightly. "I do not care if I get married in this very dress I wear now or if anyone besides Ben Weston shows up or if I spend my honeymoon in a barn. I am getting married Sunday!" I exclaimed, smiling and surprising Ben with a passionate kiss.

Keane laughed and left the room as Georgie threw up her hands in the air. "Oh, you're going to be a lot of help," she complained, but I didn't care. Nothing else mattered but being Ben's wife.

My mother was beside herself, complaining that my oldest two sisters had done the very same thing to her with their weddings, forcing her to plan in a week's time. She had been relying on me to be the sensible one.

But my father smiled and shook his head. "There is no getting Ben to wait until June. If you want to see her wed in a church, best let her marry this Sunday," he told my mother and then chuckled.

My parents had always told us that God had given each of us Andley girls a special gift: Georgiana could bake like no other, Celia was our hostess and party planner extraordinaire, Genevieve was gifted in piano, Augusta could sing like an angel, and I ...well I still wasn't for certain what I was good at, except winning at card games and speaking my mind.

But by that evening, our parlor was full of friends, thanks to my sister Celia. She had rushed to gather up women who she knew would be willing to help with whatever needed to be done.

She quickly took assessment of the most pressing needs and frowned at seeing my wedding ring quilt only half done.

Soon the soft banter and conversations of my friends and family filled the air as we sat together, sewing the intricate pieces of fabric together. I was so touched to have them all there, each one giving a part of themselves for Ben and me. Georgie would make my wedding cake, Mormor would help me sew a new dress, Genevieve would play the piano at the wedding, and Augusta would sing. Then Millie and Eleanor would go with me to Ben's house to see what things were needed to start our new lives together.

"It is a nice house, Valynn, but it is empty, completely empty. He doesn't even have a proper bed!" Millie laughed.

I frowned. This might be harder than I thought. I was but a mere farmer's daughter, but I was quite spoiled to a nice feather bed. I had a few things collected in my hope chest but mostly tea towels, linens and doilies. I had never been one to sit and sew for a future marriage like my sisters all had. I lived more in the moment, I suppose you could say. And now, due to the lack of my planning, I just might find myself sleeping on the hard floor once I married.

By the time everyone left late that night, my wedding ring quilt was finished.

I stood back admiring the colors and how it all came together so beautifully. Mere fabric scraps, bits and pieces of materials I had been collecting since my early teenage years, now all blended together for a purpose. I had never truly understood as I had collected these bits of fabric, that each tiny piece represented a piece of me, of my life, and that they would someday go into a quilt that would keep me and my husband warm. I suddenly found myself crying.

Mother smiled and hugged me closely. "I am losing another baby," she whispered, and I couldn't help but hug her even tighter.

I wouldn't be just across the fields like Georgie was. I would live a good five miles away. It was a bittersweet moment standing in the cozy parlor of my childhood home, just my mother and I, the fire crackling, my wedding quilt displayed on the frame. I would cherish that moment for years to come, I was certain.

The next day found us packing and sorting through my things.

"Where do you want these to go?" Genevieve asked, holding up a stack of novels.

I sighed. I didn't know what to take with me to my new home. I smiled and pointed to the small bureau in my room.

She laughed. "You aren't taking anything, Valynn!" she complained.

I shrugged. I couldn't explain it, but these things felt as if they belonged here, at Andley Farms, here in my childhood room. I suddenly felt fearful. Was this a bad omen of things to come? Why couldn't I pack my things and send them on over to Weston Farms?

"Mother said Ben is waiting for you in the parlor!" Augusta said, rushing in.

My heart nearly stopped. It was terribly early. We had all risen over an hour early to work on getting me packed and getting our chores done.

I looked down, I hadn't even dressed yet. I quickly tied my frilly pink flannel robe and rushed down into the parlor.

I smiled as my eyes met Ben's. He smiled tenderly, a wistful look on his face. "What?" I asked, suddenly afraid I looked a mess with my hair down to my waist and in my dressing robe.

"I have never seen your hair down, at least, not since we were children. It is beautiful, Valynn. You are beautiful," he whispered to me.

I blushed and thanked him, my stomach fluttering wildly to think he would see me like this every morning starting on Monday.

"I am leaving on the next train to Morrowville. It leaves in half an hour, I must hurry," he said, pulling me close.

My heart stopped. "Leaving?" I managed to croak out.

He smiled mischievously. "It has been brought to my attention that we do not have a proper bed, nor do I have a sofa to sit on. I do not have time to order them from Larkins Mercantile," Ben explained, but I still couldn't breathe. "I am going into Morrowville to buy furnishings.

I wish I could take you with me. I will only buy a few things, and once planting is done, perhaps we will take a small wedding trip, and you can pick out what you like," Ben said, kissing my forehead.

"So, you're not leaving for good, just for today?" I asked, relieved.

Ben smiled and pulled me even closer. "I could never leave you, Valynn. I will be back tomorrow on the afternoon train. Nearly two days away from you will do me in, I am afraid," he whispered.

I clung to him and sighed, "I love you, Ben Weston. And you had best be on that afternoon train, or you shall face my wrath, and it isn't pretty," I seriously.

Ben laughed warmly. "There isn't one thing about you, Valynn Andley, that isn't beautiful."

I had heard those words before, from Dr. McCray, but it meant so much more to me coming from Ben. "Yes, well, you haven't seen my temper since the day you threw those frogs on me. The grown up and angry Valynn is quite a monster," I assured him.

He kissed me lightly. "Well, I will miss you, my monster," he teased, and I playfully slapped his arm.

He quickly left to catch his train, and I wanted to cry. He already felt so far away. I didn't need furniture; I needed Ben to stay here beside me.

But Mother quickly hushed my tears and rushed me to eat so we could ride into town to pick out fabric for my wedding dress. I was to be at Kenrick farms just after dinner so Mormor could start sewing. Everything was happening so fast. I liked fast, but I needed Ben close. I needed to know he would still be here come Sunday. Somehow, picturing him on a train so far from me made me worry something would happen to burst this bubble of happiness I found myself.

When we arrived at the mercantile, my mother and sisters and I greeted the Larkins and headed back to the fabrics.

"Well, Valynn, this time it is your turn. Celia had a pink dress, and Georgie had white with blue flowers. What color would you like your dress to be?" Mother asked as she searched through the bolts.

I smiled, for I had always pictured myself in an elegant satin gown with an enormous train and bustle. I knew it was not practical, and like Celia and Georgie's, my dress would need to be used as a Sunday dress as well. It was March now, not quite spring, but I decided I would like a spring dress. There were always a great many spring and summer socials and barn dances; it made more sense to me to choose a lighter material. "Let's find something for a spring dress," I said decisively.

Mother quickly agreed that was wise. My sisters were a great help, lifting up various bolts to choose from, but the choices seemed overwhelming.

Then I saw the perfect fabric, and I gasped in delight. "Oh, Mother! This is it." I said, lifting it up. It was a pale green with clusters of pale pink roses.

"Oh, Valynn! How lovely," Mother said, sighing as she knew this was the one.

We quickly picked out a pale pink piping and white tulle for the underlayment. I wanted white ruffles to lie on top of the tulle with a pale pink sash. Augusta found a lovely pink satin and matching buttons, and we were done.

"Oh, Valynn, this is beautiful. A new dress?" Mrs. Larkin asked with a smile.

I nodded. "My wedding dress; I am marrying Ben Weston this Sunday. Please spread the word. The reception follows at Kenrick Farms," I said, smiling brightly.

"My... but that was quick. We certainly will tell everyone we see," Mrs. Larkin said, winking at me.

I wasn't for certain what she meant by her wink, but I was for certain I didn't like it at all. "Well, we wanted to plan a few weeks out, but Pastor Crawley is leaving for three weeks to visit his mother. We didn't want another Pastor to marry us since we have both known Pastor Crawley our entire lives. Our options were to wait until June or marry this Sunday. We didn't want to wait," I said, shrugging.

Georgie was right- people would wonder at our rushing things. I stared at the nosy store clerk. She had always been prone to gossip, but never had it been about me. I nearly wanted to slap the dark bun off the top of her pointy head.

"Of course, I was young once, I understand. And you will be there to help Ben with the planting. I am certain he will be happy to have your help and company," she said, cutting my lovely fabric.

I nodded, praying she kept her nose out of our affairs. She knew me, everyone in Crawford knew me. I had always been impetuous. Why should my hasty marriage surprise anyone?

Just then the door swung open, the bell rang, and I looked over to find Dr. McCray standing in the doorway. He stared at me as if he had seen a ghost. I nodded at him curtly and returned my attention back to Mrs. Larkin.

"Here you go, Valynn. You will make a beautiful bride. I will be sure and tell everyone to be at church this Sunday and Kenrick Farms following," Mrs. Larkin said, and my cheeks turned bright red. Dr. McCray *would* have to be in the store at that very moment. I held my breath as we turned to leave with my purchases.

He purposefully stepped into my path and greeted me. "Hello, Valynn. Did I hear you are getting married?" he asked softly, his green eyes haunting and full of pain as they searched mine.

I nodded… my heart racing. "This Sunday," I said in return, just to let him know, so he wouldn't show up for church.

"I wish you happiness, Valynn. I am afraid I will be out of town this Sunday, but tell Ben I wish you both the best," he said formally.

I thanked him and left quickly. Once we were in the buggy, my mother sighed in relief. "Oh, of all the people to come in and of all times!" she said, shaking her head in anxiety.

I sighed. "I think it was good he heard it; he once asked me to never invite him to my wedding, said he couldn't bear it. Now he knows, and he can avoid church this Sunday," I said, whispering a prayer for Dr. McCray and Ava.

"Oh! How terribly sad, Valynn," my mother said, driving the horses towards home.

I nodded, it was terribly sad for Dr. McCray *and* his wife. But I told myself I did not have to feel guilty, for I could not control Dr. McCray's feelings or his decisions. The good Lord knew I had trouble enough with my own.

Chapter Eight

I saddled my father's mare and rode over to Kenrick Farms with my fabrics and the latest styled pattern for my dress. I was beyond excited to begin sewing my dress. It made my wedding seem more real to me, assuring me that it would happen despite my fears this day. I walked into the kitchen and called out to Georgie.

"In the parlor, Valynn," she called back.

I smiled and rushed in, anxious to show her my fabric and gasped. The parlor was full of my friends and their mothers as well as a few women from church.

"Surprise!" Georgie and Celia called at the same time.

I squealed with delight, causing everyone to laugh.

"Welcome to your impromptu wedding shower," Celia announced.

I heard the back door open, and turned to see it was my mother and younger sisters. I grinned and shook my finger. "You knew of this?" I accused.

She smiled and shrugged. "Why do you think I have hurried you all morning, Valynn?" she asked, hugging both my sisters and sitting on the sofa where Millie had saved her a seat.

"Come, Valynn, you sit here. We all have gifts for you; most of them are quite practical since you gave us no time," Celia said, taking over.

Tears filled my eyes as I opened quart jars of various preserves, canned peaches, canned apples, and green beans. Next, I opened a lovely blue floral apron and a set of beautifully embroidered pillow cases. I could hardly believe these women were giving me of their best household items. I was beyond touched.

"My gift to you and Ben is a clean house," Millie giggled. "I scrubbed Ben's house from top to bottom for you, Valynn, and believe me, it needed it. Oh, these bachelors!" she said, rolling her eyes.

I hugged her closely and thanked her. She would be a wonderful sister-in-law.

Eleanor gifted me a large braided rug in blues and browns. I was in awe of its beauty and thanked her, knowing she must have worked on it all winter and most likely for her own home. "Well, you may have to sit on it if Ben doesn't get you some kind of furnishings," she giggled.

"Ben is in Morrowville as we speak, buying a few things," I admitted.

"Oh! You are so brave to allow him to leave you so close to your wedding," one of the women said. I was rather surprised she had mentioned such a thing.

"She is indeed! I would never have allowed Wilfred to leave so close to our wedding," another woman said.

I swallowed hard. It was bad enough that I had felt apprehensive about Ben's hasty departure, but these women were making it much worse.

"Oh, come now, you are scaring, Valynn. Ben was beside himself thinking of Valynn sleeping on a separate cot than his. He will return and with lovely new furniture. How lucky you are, Valynn," Millie said, rescuing me.

I thanked her, but suddenly, I had a deep fear in my heart: what if something happened to Ben, what if he didn't return?

"Come ladies, we have cake and tea in the dining room. Valynn?" Georgie called, bringing me out of my despair.

I tried to smile and nod. I tended to be dramatic at times, and this was surely one of them.

I smiled as I sat listening to my married friends and their mothers tell stories of their weddings, honeymoons, and early years of marriage. They shared with me the hard lessons learned, the fun times they cherished, and the prayers one must pray as the trials of life came.

I found myself in tears again. This was the part I hated about being in love... the tears it seemed to bring to my eyes continually. I listened to their words of wisdom, and I locked their advice safely in my heart. I wanted to be a good wife. I wanted Ben to be happy, more than anything. I knew we would face hard times, everyone did. I just prayed I could be his helpmeet and that somehow, I could be a comfort to him and help carry his burdens when needed. It was all quite serious, these life matters. But I felt ready, I truly did. Now I just needed Ben to hurry home!

That night I fell into a fitful sleep; a nightmare plagued me. It was Dr. McCray, and he was telling me Ben was gone. His green eyes were tormented, and he kept telling me that he loved me, that Ben was gone, and we could marry now. He was dragging me down the aisle of our little country church, and I was crying for Ben, not knowing why he had left me. There were slimy frogs everywhere on the pews and floor and every step I took they jumped at me, mocking me. Dr. McCray was kicking them angrily with his boot, and I was terrified. No matter how hard I tried to get away from him, I couldn't. He was too strong and quite determined. I had never been so frightened. I tried pleading with him, but he assured me over and over that I could love him again. That he loved me. That we were meant to be together.

"Valynn!" I heard my mother say sternly.

I opened my eyes and looked around, terrified. My heart was racing, and I could barely breathe. It was dark, but I was at home, in my room.

"What is it, Darling?" she asked.

"He...he has ruined it all," I cried out.

She looked concerned. "Who has ruined what?" she asked, feeling my forehead for a fever.

"Dr. McCray, he will not leave me alone, he has done something to Ben. There were frogs everywhere...he was kicking them," I wept.

Mother pulled me into her embrace. "It was just a dream, Darling. You're under too much stress planning this wedding so quickly. I feared it would do you in. Dr.

McCray did wish you well and seemed civil in the mercantile," she said tenderly.

"It was so real, Mother," I whispered.

She smiled. "Even the frogs?" she asked with a giggle.

I knew it must sound funny to her, but to me, it was still so real. A sense of fear like I had never felt before enveloped me, and I struggled to go back to sleep. I lay awake for hours praying for Ben, for his safety, and for Dr. McCray to fall in love with his wife... and quickly.

I spent the next day at Kenrick Farms sewing with Mormor on my new dress.

"You are terribly quiet today, Valynn. What is wrong?" Georgie asked me, concerned.

I shook my head, I was beyond exhausted, having been awake most of the night after my nightmare, praying for Ben, and worrying if he would return this afternoon as promised.

"You aren't having seconds thoughts are you?" Mormor asked, pausing in her sewing.

"Oh, no! Nothing like that; I suppose I am just worried about Ben," I admitted with a sigh.

Georgie and Mormor both smiled. "You know, Valynn, you have to put your trust in God. Have you not admitted to me how he has had His hand in this relationship every second of the way?" she asked tenderly.

I nodded.

"God doesn't want us to live in fear. He wants us to trust in him. I guarantee you, Ben will be in the parlor after supper tonight, dying to see you," Georgie assured me.

I thanked her and took in a deep breath. "I had no idea it hurt so much to love someone," I said, shaking my head.

Both women just grinned at me; of course, they both knew it better than I did. "Wait until you become a mother, for that is when the true pain of love comes. And not just in childbirth but in loving something so much that it hurts physically. Jori is cutting her first teeth, and I swear I haven't cried so much since Keane and I first married," Georgie said tenderly.

I smiled. I couldn't wait to be a mother. I prayed God blessed Ben and me with a house full of babies. I felt giddy thinking that this time next year, I might possibly be rocking a baby of my own. Would he or she have Ben's brown eyes and hair or my blue eyes and blonde hair? I didn't care either way; I could hardly wait to start our future together. I looked over at the clock on the fireplace mantle, silently counting down the hours until Ben's train pulled into Crawford.

I left Kenrick Farms rather late, but I was thrilled with how close my wedding dress was to being done. Tomorrow it would be completely finished. Mormor had done a beautiful job, and I couldn't wait for my mother and younger sisters to see it.

I looked over at the sun that was now setting. My mother would be worried if I didn't hurry, and Ben's train should arrive in town within the hour. I couldn't wait to see him; he had been gone less than two days, but I missed him terribly. I was trying not to worry about Ben and our coming marriage, but it was difficult. I couldn't explain it, this strange and foreboding feeling I had. Georgie assured me it was just pre-wedding jitters. But in my mind and heart, it was a true sense of fear. Not a fear of marrying Ben. I felt completely in God's will that I was to be his wife. No, this was like an unspoken whisper of doom that something would happen, and I would lose this joy I had found with Ben.

I was lost in thought when suddenly I heard a horse and rider approaching me from the wooded area that sat between Kenrick Farms and my father's farm. I felt a little alarmed. No one ever rode this path except for my family. I was suddenly worried that something might have happened to one of my sisters.

I pulled my mare, Lady, to a halt and then held my breath as I realized it was none other than Niall McCray. He pulled his horse up beside me and smiled.

"Dr. McCray, what brings you out here?" I asked, trying to sound calm. Anyone besides my family would have used the dirt road between the two farms. Dr. McCray had no business being out here. I sat, wishing I would have had Keane ride home with me or Henry even, but what would I have had to fear? Now I had to wonder if Dr. McCray had been waiting on me.

"Good evening, Valynn," he greeted with a smile.

I nodded curtly, not wishing to speak to him anymore than I had to. He looked filthy and disheveled, but in his line of work I supposed that was normal.

"I needed to speak with you, and well, Keane has forbidden me to speak to you on Kenrick Farms property," he said, frowning.

I was rather surprised to hear that. Keane had indeed punched Niall, but Niall had apologized for his early morning interruption and had seemed more himself the last time I had seen him at Kenrick Farms and in the mercantile. My heart raced wildly now, for this confirmed my suspicion. He had indeed waited for me to leave Kenrick Farms; he had been watching me. *I could hardly breathe.* "Ride home with me. I am already past due, and Mother and Father will be worried. I will speak to you there," I said, kicking my horse to start.

But to my horror, Dr. McCray grabbed the reins, stopping me. "I need to speak to you here, Valynn. Just for a moment. Please," he said, his green eyes pleading.

I tried to calm myself; I truly didn't believe Dr. McCray would hurt me. "Please, Niall; my father has most likely already left looking for me. I stayed too long with Georgie. Come and grab a cup of coffee," I urged, trying to give him a calm smile, but I knew I had failed miserably.

"Valynn, I have been beside myself since I saw you in town. Please, do not marry Ben!" he pleaded.

I could not believe the nerve of this man. My fear was edging into anger now. "Need I remind you, Dr. McCray, you are married to Ava?"

Niall's face turned dark and his green eyes stormy.

"Please God, help me," I prayed silently. Dr. McCray still held the reins to my horse.

"We can still find a way, Valynn. I will divorce her, and we can leave together. My family has money; we can go back East and start our lives together. *I cannot live without you*," he said softly.

I shook my head, frightened tears threatening my eyes. "You must! You have no choice but to live without me! You chose Ava. And I am in love with Ben. I want to marry him!" I was so angry, I could hardly see straight.

"Ava tricked me, Valynn! We, you and I, were meant to be together. We had something; I know you felt it, too," he whispered desperately, as if he were in pain.

"We had nothing!" I screamed at him. "Let me go, Niall," I pleaded.

"Valynn, remember the sleigh ride and the afternoon at Kenrick Farms?" he asked me.

I shook my head, "That is all we shared, a sleigh ride, nothing more, Niall! You chose her, you chose Ava. Now go home and be a husband to her. Let her love you and make you a home, give you children, just give her a chance," I said, starting to panic now.

He shook his head. He wasn't listening. "I can't let you go, Valynn. I love you. *I will always love you*. I will not let you go, I can never let you go," he said desperately. His hands tightened on the reins to my horse and I knew he was serious.

My eyes scanned the horizon, praying someone was looking for me, anyone. "I need to go home, now, Niall. Please, just let me go home," I said, trying to reason with him.

"Valynn, you don't really love Ben! You were trying to make me jealous. *It worked*! I have been miserable since that night at the dance. Marrying him will be the biggest mistake of your life. You love me, I see it in your eyes," he said, reaching for me.

I was terrified and tried to break free from him, but Lady was spooked and both horses started to spin nervously. I was certain it was my alarm Lady sensed. I silently prayed once again for my family to come looking for me. "Niall, I do not love you! I never did! It was an attraction, but that is all! I have told you time and again, I wouldn't have you. I deserve someone who loves me and me alone! You cared for Ava; you wouldn't have kept seeing her if you didn't!" I said, trying to keep him talking, giving someone a chance to rescue me.

He shook his head angrily. "I see the love in your eyes for me, Valynn. You can deny it all you want, but it is there!" he said a bit too loudly.

My horse was near to bolt with me. Perhaps I should let her I thought to myself. *"It is fear you see in my eyes, you idiot*! Let me go, Niall. You do not want to keep me here, my father will be furious!" I warned.

"I'm not letting you go, Valynn. Not until you see and admit we were meant to be together. *Valynn, I love you so desperately,*" he said, leaning in toward me.

I put my hands up to keep him from kissing me and leaned too far over on my horse. Before I knew what happened, I fell to the ground, hard, knocking the wind from my lungs.

My horse spooked and reared into the air as Niall struggled to keep his horse and mine contained. The air had been knocked out of me, but I scrambled to my feet, and ran with everything I had toward the wooded area and toward my home.

"Valynn!" Niall yelled after me.

I turned to see him give up in frustration and slap my horse on her rump. Lady took off toward home. At least my father would see she had returned without me and would come looking for me. At least, I prayed he did.

I ran into the wooded area and was thankful it was getting quite dark by now. I could hear hooves pounding somewhere behind me, and all I could do was pray. Suddenly a Bible verse from Jeremiah 17 came to me, "For he shall be as a tree planted by the waters, and that spreadeth out her roots by the river, and shall not see when heat cometh." The woods were full of various cedar trees, tall, and full of branches down to their roots.

I ran to the largest one in my view and crawled on my knees to its base; its sticky and scratchy branches tore my dress sleeve and scratched my face. I clamped a hand over my mouth lest my frightened sobs come out and Dr. McCray hear me.

I heard him ride past me, slowly, calling my name. I trembled in fear, but luckily he passed by without seeing me, his horse having to go much slower through the brush than I had by foot.

I sat and waited. I wanted to make certain I wasn't within his range of sight before I tried to escape. There was no way I could get home without him seeing me. If he didn't see me in the fields, he would no doubt head towards Kenrick Farms. I felt trapped.

I heard things scurrying in the tree above me, and I cringed and wondered what wildlife I was sharing this haven with. I prayed it was friendly, and I prayed it was not frogs.

A light rain began to fall, and I groaned inwardly. At least I had *some* shelter in the middle of this massive tree, but soon I was shivering from the cool March wind, the cold and damp ground now seeping through my skirts. Would Niall have hurt me? Had I overreacted? He had already forced a kiss on me with Keane near us both. If he hadn't held onto my horse's reins, perhaps I wouldn't have been so frightened. But he had no right trying to kiss me, he was married. His lack of reasoning was frightening me. His vow, "*I will not let you go,*" pounded in my head so heavily that I stayed beneath the tree not knowing if he truly meant to harm me. He had ignored my pleas to follow me home and to let me go. But, he had sent Lady on towards home and he wouldn't have if he intended to harm me, I tried reasoning with myself. I knew I had to leave this tree soon and get to warmth.

I went to scoot out from beneath the tree when another Scripture came to me, "Rest in the Lord and wait patiently for Him; fret not thyself because of him who prospereth in his way, because of the man who bringeth wicked devices to pass." And then another, "Be still and know that I am God." I worked my way back under the tree to its trunk and leaned against it for warmth. My heart told me to sit still, that God was with me, directing me to stay.

A measure of peace flooded over me, and I was able to pray for Niall McCray. I prayed that God would wake him somehow, that he would leave me alone and end this torture to himself. I prayed for my Father or Keane to find me quickly. I had never felt so cold.

I must have dozed off and was startled when something woke me. I kept alert now, hearing noises that I could not determine for certain. I knew I was not alone in this tree, and with the wind now howling and the rain falling harder, I prayed fervently for a rescue. I was soaked clean through now. How long had I been out here alone? I was certain Lady had returned home by now, and I prayed Father had found her and was out looking for me. My mind raced with fear, and I had to pray hard against it. The cold was now affecting my own reasoning as I struggled to keep my wits about me.

I sat shivering violently for what must have been another hour. I was so cold I could hardly feel my hands, and my teeth chattered so loudly I feared if Niall was waiting on me, he would surely hear me. I strained to listen for horses, voices, any sign that my father or Keane was looking for me. But the noises of the night were whispering eerily to me as I sat in the darkness alone, knowing somewhere out there was a crazed veterinarian who thought he was in love with me, who couldn't seem to leave me alone. Why was this happening to me?

"Ben," I whispered as I shivered. Had his train arrived safely? Had Niall McCray somehow hurt him? My dream was all too vivid in my mind as I huddled beneath this tree.

"Ben, I need you," I whispered, feeling so very tired I could hardly stay awake. If my teeth weren't chattering so hard, I most likely would have fallen back to sleep by now. I lay my head against the large trunk of the tree. What was taking my father so long? Surely he didn't just assume I was still with Georgie?

If I left the security of the tree, I doubted I could see to make it home. I couldn't even see my hand before my face now. And what if Niall was waiting just at the woods edge! He would see me if I tried to make it home or back towards Kenrick Farms. I truly was trapped. Why was this happening to me just two days before my wedding to Ben? My back ached, my legs ached, and soon I closed my eyes as darkness overtook me.

Something warm was on my head and then my shoulder. I was so cold, was I dreaming? I struggled to open my eyes. It was so dark. Were my eyes even open? I sat up, panicked as something scratched my face. Then something moved on me. My hand was in the wet dirt and leaves, and I screamed as two small beady eyes glowed near my face.

It was all coming back to me; I was under a tree, in the woods, hiding from Dr. McCray. I looked around but could see nothing, it was so dark. The object that had been on my shoulder ran up the tree and I realized it was just a squirrel. I couldn't help but cry.

"Valynn!" A man yelled.

"Oh God, please, please help me," I whispered, wrapping my arms around the tree trunk and pressing my body to it. *He had found me.*

"Valynn! Valynn!" I heard, and now I struggled to make sense of it; it had sounded like an echo far away. Now it seemed to call to me from every direction. I didn't move. I forced myself to stop crying by biting my bottom lip so hard I tasted blood. He knew I was in the woods; it wouldn't take long to find me. I didn't even know how long I had been out here. Why hadn't my father come for me?

"Valynn," I heard much closer, and I held my breath. I could hear footsteps now, the crunching of the leaves and twigs beneath heavy boots. *He was getting closer.* I was near hysteria.

"I heard her scream; she has to be close," I heard.

"Ben?" I whispered.

"Valynn," he called, and I sensed he was near, *my Ben*.

I suddenly found I couldn't move, I was too cold, too cramped.

"Are you certain it was this direction?" I heard another man ask. Was it Isaac?

"Ben!" I screamed with all that I had, but it came out much weaker than I wished.

"Valynn! I hear you, where are you, Sweetheart?" Ben asked, panicked.

"Ben!" I screamed again and tried to work my legs out in front of me. I would scoot out on my backside from beneath this tree if I had to.

"Valynn, where are you? Keep talking to me, come on, Sweetheart, talk to me," he pleaded, and I could hear his footsteps running now.

"I am in here, Ben, in the large cedar tree." I was so tired and weak. I rolled onto my stomach and pushed with my feet as I dug into the earth with my hands, slowly inching across the ground.

"Which tree, Valynn, which tree, Sweetheart?" he asked, and I had to smile, which tree indeed, I was in a thick wood with hundreds of cedar trees, and it was pitch dark.

"Valynn, keep talking to me...Valynn," he pleaded, and I could hear the urgency in his voice.

"Here. Over here," I struggled to say as my head tried to push through the tree. My hands dug into the dirt trying to pull myself out. Was I frozen? Why wasn't my body cooperating?

"Ben, she is here, over here, Ben," I heard the other man say, and I looked up to see a lantern rushing toward me.

The man knelt down, and I tried not to scream; I would die if it were Niall McCray. But it was only Isaac, Isaac Stein, my friend and old beau.

"Dear heavens, Valynn!" Isaac said, lifting my head and shoulders into his arms.

I heard heavy footfalls, and soon Ben's warm brown eyes were staring back at me in the dim lantern light.

"Thank you, God, thank you! Valynn, Sweetheart, talk to me!" he pleaded, pulling me into his arms.

My head fell against his, and I all I could whisper was his name. "*Ben.*"

It seemed I would dream forever. One moment I was dancing with Ben at Kenrick Farms, the next I was baking cookies with Genevieve and Augusta. One moment I could hear a baby cry, and the next I was running from Niall McCray's tormented green eyes. I felt things crawling on me, lifting me; I felt extreme coldness and then terrible heat that I could not escape. I heard voices whispering. I heard a soft weeping that made me cry as well.

I ran and ran and crawled through the dirt begging him to leave me alone, to go away. *Just go away*, I begged him. And then I heard arguing, scuffling, men shouting loudly and women screaming. I tried to sit up, but the room was spinning, the bed was spinning. Why was I still in bed?

Cool hands pushed me down gently, a cool rag smoothed across my face. Someone was humming, and it soothed me. The heat finally resided, and I slept. It seemed as if I would sleep forever.

"Drink this, Valynn," I heard a muffled voice say over and over. I shook my head no, suddenly remembering that the last time I had heard that voice, a nasty and bitter tasting liquid soon followed; I wanted no more of it.

"Come on, Valynn, you must drink this," I heard again.

I shook my head and slapped at hands that were on my arms.

"Valynn, Sweetheart, you must drink this, come now, Love, drink this for me." It was Ben's voice.

My eyes fluttered furiously as I struggled to wake; I needed to see Ben. "Ben," I tried to say.

"She knows it is you, Ben," I heard, and thought it sounded like Georgie.

"Valynn, *my Love*," Ben said, kissing my hand.

I fought until I could see the dim light of a candle on a table. I turned my head and saw him, fuzzy brown eyes filled with tears. I tried to smile, but my face felt as if it weighed too much to move.

"Dr. Anderson," I heard Ben call out.

I grabbed his hand; I didn't want him to leave me. "Ben," I tried to say again.

Suddenly he was kissing my face, and I felt his tears hit my cheeks. Why was Ben crying?

I saw Georgie, my mother, my father, Genevieve, Augusta, and Celia rushing in behind Dr. Anderson, their eyes all filled with tears, their faces smiling.

"Valynn, I need you to drink this. I know it is terrible, but you have been very sick. You must get better. For me, Valynn, you must get better for me, my love," Ben said, lifting a cup to my lips.

Dr. Anderson lifted my shoulders and head, and I sipped the bitter liquid and was thankful for a sip of lukewarm tea that shortly followed. Their voices became muffled once again, and I fought the sleep that threatened to overtake me. I didn't want to lose Ben. I clung to his hand as tightly as I could. His warm hands entwined with mine. His lips kissed my hands over and over. *He was here, and I was safe.*

I awoke with a start, my heart racing, and I was wet with sweat. I looked around my room, panicked. I had been dreaming. I had dreamt I was under a cedar tree, cold and afraid, hiding.

I breathed deeply as if I hadn't breathed air into my lungs before, and then I coughed. The room was bright, and suddenly Ben was looking over me, and there was my mother, and then Dr. Anderson. It frightened me. "What are you all looking at?" I asked, but my throat crackled like an old woman's.

Laughter filled the room, and I couldn't help but think I must still be dreaming until Ben knelt beside the bed and I realized Ben was in my room. "Ben," I gasped.

His brown eyes twinkled, and he kissed my cheek tenderly.

Dr. Anderson was listening to my breathing with a stethoscope, and I found myself swatting his hands away. This brought on more laughter.

Ben took my hands in his, and suddenly this all seemed very familiar, warm hands holding mine, my slapping at something cold on me.

"You have been very sick, Valynn," my mother said, bringing me a glass of cool water.

Ben lifted my shoulders up, and my mother put the glass to my lips as I drank in deeply of the water.

"Not too much, Valynn," Dr. Anderson warned gently.

I could no longer sit up. What had happened to me? "How long have I been sick?" I asked, my voice sounding strange to me.

"For three days," Ben said tenderly.

I gasped in shock as tears filled my eyes. "Our wedding?" I asked softly. Tears streamed down my cheeks; *I had missed my own wedding*. Why? Then it hit me hard, memories of that night, Niall McCray, being so cold and afraid, the squirrel on my head, the scratches and dirt. It hadn't been a dream, it had been real.

"It is all right, Valynn, we will still marry! The important thing is you're getting well. You have had us all scared to death," Ben said, kissing my hand.

I could see the concern and affection in his eyes. "Oh, Ben!" I cried.

"Shh, it is all right. I am just so thankful you're getting better. I love you, Valynn. I promise as soon as you have recovered, we will marry," he whispered.

I couldn't stop crying. "He ruined it, just as I dreamed he would. *I hate him, I hate him,*" I said, growing hysterical now.

Mother looked concerned and quickly tried to calm me, but I wouldn't listen.

Ben sat on the bed beside me, pulling my head to his chest, kissing the top of my head tenderly. "You mustn't worry, you are safe now, and he cannot hurt you. I am here, I will always be here. I will never leave you again, I promise," he whispered over and over to me.

"He ruined my wedding, he begged me not to marry you, and he made certain I couldn't," I said, crying into Ben's chest. I felt Ben stiffen beneath me, and Dr. Anderson and my mother looked concerned.

"Valynn, you must calm down, or I will have to give you something to make you sleep. You have suffered trauma and illness, so you need to rest and be at peace," Dr. Anderson said softly.

"I will get her some chamomile tea," my mother said, rushing away.

"Valynn, please do not cry, Sweetheart, please," Ben pleaded, emotionally.

I realized this must be hard on him as well. I hugged him closely and closed my eyes. I felt safe in his embrace, but I was still very angry with Niall McCray. *I hated him.*

Chapter Nine

It would be three more days before I would know exactly what happened that night, six days ago, when I had hidden in fear from Dr. McCray.

It was on this day that I could finally sit up in bed, and that I could control my emotions and tears. I had not been allowed visitors except for my mother, father, sisters, and Ben. Dr. Anderson and Ben had not left my side, both sleeping on cots in my room, my mother sleeping beside me in my bed.

But on this day, I would wait no longer to hear the details. I was angry, and although I was controlling it the best I could, I needed closure. I needed to move past this fear. I didn't know if anyone knew what Dr. McCray had done or why I had been hiding in the woods, but I couldn't help but fear he would still come for me. "So, tell me, how did you find me?" I asked Ben.

He looked uncomfortable and sighed, but once Dr. Anderson nodded to him, he spoke. "My train arrived around six; Drew and Millie picked me up at the station and helped me get the furniture home in the wagon. We had just unloaded the bed when Keane arrived; your father had ridden to Kenrick Farms looking for you. On the way, he met Dr. McCray. Niall was hysterical and your father couldn't get him to make sense, but he knew your horse arriving home without you was somehow Niall's doing. Niall had been looking for you and was crazy with worry that you would be hurt because of him because of what he did. Your father rode to get Henry and Keane. Keane thought perhaps you had tried to make it to Weston Farms, to me. He told us you were missing, and that Niall was looking for you. Valynn, I went crazy," he paused.

My heart sank; surely he hadn't killed Niall? I put a hand over my mouth as he continued.

"Of course Drew and I took off like wild boars through the woods. Georgie had taken off into town like a banshee to find the sheriff. Isaac was in town coming out of the diner, and she told him you were missing in the woods and that Niall was out there as well. The sheriff came out with Isaac, and when I got to where Niall was, I lost control, Valynn, and I beat him; I couldn't stop beating him. He kept saying your name over and over and how he caused this," Ben said emotionally.

"You killed him?" I asked in a whisper.

He shook his head no. "No, he is alive," Ben said, looking at Dr. Anderson who listened solemnly.

I could hardly breathe. Niall was alive, but how alive? By the way Ben spoke, it didn't sound good.

"The sheriff took Niall away. Your father, Henry, Keane, Drew, Isaac and I split up. Isaac and I went back into the woods. We searched for over two hours. I was just about to give up and move to another area when I heard you scream. I had walked right past you twice, calling to you, but never knew you were hidden under that tree," he said, swallowing hard and then suddenly wiping away a tear.

"Ben," I whispered, taking his hand in mine.

He shook his head, trying to be strong, but it was this broken emotion that ensured me that he truly loved me, loved me enough to fight for me although I saw how it had hurt him to do so.

"We heard you scream," he started again and shook his head, once again struggling to gain control of his emotions.

My heart ached for him. "I woke up and was scared; there was a squirrel on my head," I said, remembering the feeling of-that-thing crawling on me.

Ben looked surprised, and then tried to fight a smile through his tears. "Well, I asked God to help us find you; I suppose if he used a donkey in the Bible, he can use a squirrel, too," he said, kissing my hand tenderly.

"You heard me, and you were calling to me, but you were so cold, your voice so soft. I knew you were hurt, and I was out of my head with worry. Isaac and I split up and listened for you, and then suddenly you stopped calling to me. Isaac found you; you had managed to crawl a little ways out from beneath that tree. I have never been so frightened in my entire life, nor more thankful as when Isaac found you. You were wet and freezing and running a fever by the time we got to you. For three days you fought that fever, and we watched as you struggled. We prayed God would let us keep you," he said, tears now streaming down his cheeks.

Dr. Anderson cleared his throat. "Valynn, we need to know what Niall did to you. He was so distraught, and no one could get him to make sense. When he was brought to me, he was injured and couldn't speak. We need to know, did he.....did he take you by force, you know, intimately?" Dr. Anderson asked tenderly.

I heard my mother start to sob in the corner.

"No, no, he didn't touch me," I said, taking a deep breath.

Ben sighed in relief, and my mother praised God softly where she sat in the chair near my bed.

"I was frightened; I didn't know what he would do. He found me; he had been watching me, waiting on me. He knew I had been at Kenrick Farms, and he knew Keane would not allow him to speak with me there. He knew when I left," I said, shivering.

Ben took my hands in his and bowed his head over them. I could feel his warm face on my skin and knew he struggled to control his emotions.

"I told him I was running late, that Father had more than likely left to find me. He said he couldn't go on without me and that he would divorce Ava and we could leave together and marry. I told him no, told him that I loved Ben; I wanted to marry Ben. He reminded me of the sleigh ride and the afternoon we spent at Kenrick Farms. He told me that we had something between us, that he knew I felt it too."

Ben stiffened and held my hands tightly.

"Go on, Valynn," Dr. Anderson urged.

"I was scared by then, and I told him that we had nothing and to let me go. But he grabbed my reins and held them. He wanted me to hear what he had to say. He begged me not to marry Ben; he said he couldn't live without me. He said he would never let me go. He wouldn't listen to me. I begged him to let me go home. But he wouldn't listen. He wouldn't let go of my reins. He leaned in to kiss me, and I panicked. I put my hands up quickly to block his advance and leaned too far away from him and fell from my horse to the ground. The horses spooked, and Niall struggled to control them. I remember running as fast as I could. I looked behind me as Niall screamed for me to stop; he was having trouble controlling both horses. I kept running into the woods." I paused to look at Ben.

His handsome face was tense. He was struggling with his anger. I didn't want to upset him.

"Did Niall chase after you?" Dr. Anderson asked.

I nodded. "God brought a Scripture to me, and I saw the tree. I climbed in underneath and waited and prayed for help," I said, softly crying now. "He rode by me, calling for me, but I was too afraid. I didn't want him to see where I was. He may not have meant me any harm, but I felt such fear. His eyes were tormented. He was dirty and disheveled. He just kept saying that he would not let me go," I said, breaking down now.

Ben sat beside me on the bed and once again held me in his arms. My mother wept softly in her chair, and Dr. Anderson nodded.

"You made a wise choice, Valynn. God was with you. When the sheriff came, he found two train tickets to Davenport in Niall's coat pocket; they were for that very same night. We think Niall planned on taking you and running away with you, with or without your consent. I cannot say if he would have hurt you or not, but he was intent on having you," Dr. Anderson said solemnly.

I wiped my eyes and Ben held me close. "You said he is alive?" I said softly.

Dr. Anderson nodded and then smiled. "Ben whooped the feathers out of him, but he will live. He probably wishes he wouldn't for a while with those broke ribs," Dr. Anderson said with a weak smile.

I felt Ben stiffen beside me, and I hugged him closely, taking his hands in mine, and for the first time, noticing how bruised and cut his hands were. I kissed them tenderly, for he had done his best to protect me.

"Valynn, Dr. McCray is gone. You need not worry anymore," Ben whispered.

I looked up shocked. "Gone?" I asked, daring to be relieved.

Dr. Anderson nodded. "When Fredrick Stein heard that Niall had been to Kenrick Farms, asking you to run away with him, then about this, and that he was the cause of you being hurt and missing, he personally escorted Niall and Ava back to North Hampton where Niall has family. Niall will be closely monitored in house arrest until this is cleared up. But Fredrick said under no circumstances is he to return to Crawford. If he is to practice his profession, he will have to do it elsewhere. Niall's farm is up for sale, and the sheriff just awaits your side of the story before they decide how to handle Niall from here," Dr. Anderson sighed.

I nodded and laid my head against Ben's chest. I couldn't think of it just yet. I needed time to pray.

A few days later I was strong enough to make it into the parlor. The scratches on my face had nearly healed and I was able to take a nice long bath and then visit with my sisters, who all awaited me, along with Eleanor and Millie in the parlor.

Dr. Anderson had returned to town, and I had finally convinced Ben, just that morning, to go home. I didn't want him to leave me, but he had not slept well in over a week and a half on the cot in my room. I couldn't have him getting sick on me.

Spring plowing was soon upon us, and I knew Ben would need his strength for the coming season. We had not decided on a date for the wedding; we were just waiting for the slow process of me gaining my energy and health back. And I was as impatient as ever.

I smiled and laughed for the first time in a week and a half as I visited with my friends and hugged on my sisters. It was the best medicine I could have received. To snuggle my niece and nephew, to hear Genevieve play her latest piece on the piano, and to listen as Augusta sang to us. It was in the everyday, wonderfully familiar things in which I found the most healing. It brought a much- needed peace to my spirit.

Mother made our favorite cookies and cocoa, and we laughed into the late afternoon until they all had to leave to start supper for their families. Just as my sisters were leaving to return home, Ben arrived with Isaac.

"Ben Weston, you are supposed to be home sleeping," I said, scolding him but with a bright smile. I loved it that he couldn't stay away from me.

"I have a visitor who has been begging to see you, Valynn," he said, kissing my cheek softly. He sat next to me as Isaac sat across from us in the chair.

I smiled. "Isaac, I am so glad you have come. I have wanted to thank you for your help in finding me," I said, thankful he could still be my friend and wondering how I ever thought I could have married him a year ago.

Isaac smiled, his grey eyes twinkling with appreciation. "Seeing you well again, Valynn, is all the thanks I need. You had us worried," he said with a smile.

"I am sorry for that," I shrugged. "You know me, I always have to be bothering someone; this time I just picked a few of you," I teased.

Isaac laughed. "Yah, well don't do it again, please. That man beside you nearly came apart, nearly tore someone apart as well. I can't stand to see my best friend like that, nor can I stand to see my best girl lying scratched up in the dirt," he said, and I could see he still cared for me.

I swallowed hard and thanked him. He wasn't madly in love with me as he believed, he would soon realize that, but we would always have a bond between us, strengthened by our many years of friendship.

Isaac stayed for cake and coffee, and then left as Ben and I thanked him once again.

When we were alone in the parlor, I lay my head against Ben's shoulder. "What are you doing back, Ben? I want you to go home and get some sleep," I said tenderly.

Ben pulled me close and sighed into my hair. "Oh, Valynn, I have slept in your room for over a week now. I can't stand the thought of being five miles away from you, not hearing you breathing across the room from me. I can't sleep at my house. I need to be here with you. I can't leave you," he whispered.

I hugged him tightly. His lips found mine, and I smiled after he broke our kiss, breathless. "If you would have kissed me like that six days ago, Ben Weston, I would be much more recovered," I giggled.

Ben smiled. "Then I shall have to kiss you until you are well enough to run down that aisle at church and marry me," he teased in return.

I laughed warmly. "I can just see it now, me running towards you in my lovely new wedding dress, and you throwing a handful of frogs at me," I sighed against his shoulder. I hated to admit it, but I was exhausted.

"Frogs again? Valynn, will you never forgive me for that day so long ago?" he asked, trying to act exasperated with me.

I closed my eyes with fatigue but smiled. "I suppose I must forgive you, but I am not so good about forgetting. I will be on watch at all times with you around, Ben Weston," I teased.

He kissed the top of my head tenderly. "You will grow weary of watching, I am afraid, for I never plan to let you out of my sight again, Valynn Andley," he whispered with great emotion.

I hugged his arm more tightly, and prayed that we would never be separated, not even for a day. I loved him this much.

I lay awake in bed, replaying the past two weeks almost or what I remembered of them. Ben had not left my side, only for a few hours, and not until this very day. I smiled, for it meant so much to me. My mother lay sleeping next to me, just as she had every night since the incident. My family had taken such good care of me, making me feel safe.

I rose up on my elbow; Ben lay on a cot across the room. I smiled again, loving having him near. I didn't want him to go home, not unless I could go with him, as his wife. "*His wife,*" I whispered. If Niall McCray hadn't pulled such a stunt, I would be in my new home, beside Ben, as his wife. Angry tears filled my eyes. I hated Niall McCray! He had ruined everything. I should be Ben's wife!

I stood from bed carefully, trying not to wake my mother. I had only taken a step when Ben sat up abruptly. I sighed; it was just as I had thought: the poor man was hardly getting any rest here, worrying over me.

"Valynn, are you all right?" he whispered as I reached him.

I shook my head no as I knelt before him, next to his cot.

His eyes searched mine in the moonlit room. "What is it, Sweetheart?" he asked.

"Ben," I started, but my tears kept me from saying more.

Ben brushed my hair from my eyes tenderly. "What is it, Valynn?"

"I just needed to see you," I confessed.

He smiled sleepily, and I wondered if I could ever love him more than I did in that instant. He kissed my hand tenderly. If Niall McCray hadn't ruined things for us, I could be in my new home right now, snuggled next to Ben. I would never forgive him for this! "If we had married, if Niall hadn't.....I would be your wife, right now."

Ben gave me a sympathetic smile. "I know, Sweetheart, I know. But you're getting better. And Valynn, I would wait years to marry you, if I had to. You scared me, Sweetheart. I thought I had lost you," he whispered emotionally.

"Do you think God allowed this because we were trying to rush things too soon?" I asked.

Ben sighed and wiped a tear from my cheek. He shook his head no. "I think God's plan is still for us to wed. I think Niall McCray went crazy with not having you. He messed things up a bit. But Valynn, we will still marry, *he didn't ruin us*. I love you more than I ever have, and

Niall cannot change that, no one can." He pulled me into his embrace, and it made me cry even more.

"I hate him!" I whispered.

Ben pulled back, concern in his brown eyes. "Valynn, we cannot hate him. The Bible tells us we must pray for our enemies. I am struggling with my feelings for the man myself, but Sweetheart, we have to forgive him, pray for him, and move on," Ben whispered.

I shook my head. "He is selfish, self-serving, conniving, and....I hate him," I insisted.

Ben sighed. "I beat him, Valynn, within an inch of his life. I didn't wait to hear what happened. I didn't wait to see if he was innocent. He merely said your name, and I beat the thunder out him. Do you hate me, too? I nearly ended a man's life without waiting to learn what he had done."

I gasped. "I could never hate you, Ben! You were just trying to protect me."

"Valynn, I nearly acted as reckless as Niall. I was trying to protect you, yes. But my jealousy had a big part in my actions as well. I am not proud of what I did or how I lost control. I was out of control, Valynn, just as Niall was."

I shook my head no; I wouldn't believe Ben's actions were comparable to Niall's.

"In order for us to put this behind us, Sweetheart, we must forgive."

I sighed, knowing somehow that the words he spoke were right and full of wisdom. I had to let go of this anger I held, to let go of the fact that my wedding had been delayed. That my plans had changed against my will.

"Valynn, come to bed now," my mother said firmly, startling me.

I gasped, and Ben quickly pressed a kiss to my forehead. "I love you," he whispered.

I hugged him once more before standing. "I love you, Ben Weston. Thank you for being Godly, for being here," I whispered.

I crept back to bed feeling like a naughty child caught doing something wrong, and yet I knew we hadn't. How could Ben be so wise? He was good for me, I was certain of that.

I closed my eyes and prayed for forgiveness. I prayed for help in forgiving Niall. And I prayed for Ava, knowing this had to be difficult for her as well. I prayed that whatever was wrong with Niall, that God would heal him. And then I prayed for Ben and me. I just wanted to get married, to be his wife, to work our farm, to have babies and be blissfully happy. I fell asleep dreaming about sitting on Ben's back porch, my head on his shoulder and Yonder at our feet. *I wanted nothing more.*

The next evening, the sheriff of Crawford came to talk with me along with Isaac, Dr. Anderson, and Ben.

My hands shook nervously as I retold the story of what happened and listened once again as Ben and Dr. Anderson, and this time my father as well, gave accounts of Niall McCray's actions that night nearly two weeks ago.

"I do not know if his intentions were to harm me," I confessed. "I was frightened when he would not listen to me, when he would not let me go; that is why I hid, but I cannot tell you what his intentions were," I said softly.

Ben took my hand in his and gave me a weak smile. Sheriff Byler gave me a sympathetic smile and nodded in understanding.

I sighed heavily, determined I was going to forgive Niall McCray. "I do not wish to punish Niall any farther. I am frightened of him, but I care about Ava, and I know this has to be hard on her, as well as the Stein family. If we can enforce it to where he is never allowed on Weston Farms, Andley Farms, or Kenrick Farms, I think I will be all right with that," I said, my voice revealing my emotion.

"Father will never allow him to live here again, Valynn. It is tearing him apart that he forced Ava to marry him. But she had her part in that as well, and now she is stuck with Niall McCray. They will live in North Hampton near his parents. But, I suppose if they could return once a year for a holiday, my parents would be beholding to you. You have my word he would be watched carefully, and we would let you and Ben know before they arrived," Isaac said tenderly.

I nodded in agreement and looked to Ben.

He sighed and shrugged. "It is your decision, Valynn. Although, if he was to return, even for a holiday, and ever tried to contact you, I am afraid of what I would do to him," Ben admitted.

I took his hand in mine, knowing he was still struggling with what he had done to Niall and with his own anger toward the man.

"I promise I would watch him, Ben. But, knowing Ava, she will not return for quite some time. She is taking this very hard. She has telegraphed twice asking if Valynn is recovering," Isaac said.

Ben nodded his agreement.

The sheriff and Dr. Anderson thanked us as they left, and I was glad to finally be able to put this behind me now. There was a peace that had not been there just the day before, before I began praying for help to forgive Niall McCray.

We joined my parents and younger sisters in the dining room for dessert and coffee. Their laughter and conversation were a much-needed rescue, and soon I felt at peace and was able to relax and enjoy our evening together.

"So, when are we going to see you two married?" my mother shocked me by asking.

Ben smiled and looked to me expectantly. "I....I do not know; plowing starts in less than a week. Pastor Crawley is out of town. I suppose we should plan for some time in June," I said, knowing we had to wait until the planting season was finished.

Ben hung his head and looked like a disappointed child; it nearly broke my heart.

"You know, Sheriff Byler is authorized to perform marriages. It wouldn't be a church wedding, but Kenrick Farms would be a lovely place to marry and then a reception in the barn," Mother said, smiling.

I was shocked; my mother was suggesting I marry outside a church, by a sheriff and not Pastor Crawley.

"Of course, it is up to you both. But, Ben Weston, you are not sleeping in a cot in my daughter's room any longer. I am ready to return to my own bed. Valynn, I think the sooner you are with Ben and in your new home, the sooner you will get your strength and spirit back," she said tenderly.

Ben looked to me, hopeful, but I knew he wanted me to have what I wanted, and he was worried I wanted a church wedding.

I sighed dramatically. "Well Ben Weston, what are you waiting for? Go round up that sheriff!" I said, smiling.

Ben pulled me to him and kissed me right in front of my parents.

Augusta giggled and Genevieve rolled her eyes. My parents both blushed, but I didn't care; the only thing that mattered to me was becoming Ben Weston's bride. I would marry him in a barn, outside in the front yard, or even in a creek for that matter, well....perhaps not the creek, I couldn't possibly forget about the frogs!

"When, Valynn? When can I get the sheriff?" Ben asked before he left for home.

I smiled. "How about...tomorrow night," I whispered.

Ben smiled as he leaned down to kiss me. I could hardly believe that tomorrow night, I would be Mrs. Benjamin Weston.

"It seems like forever away, especially since your mother has kicked me out of your room," he complained.

I smiled and blushed. I would miss knowing he was there. No doubt I would make one of my sister's sleep next to me this night. "One more night, Ben, and then you are stuck with me for life," I warned.

He smiled. "Promise?" he asked.

I nodded.

"I love you, Valynn Andley. I guess I had best get home and set that furniture up," he chuckled.

I laughed warmly. "Yes, you had better! I might be a farmer's daughter, but I am spoiled to a soft feather bed, Ben Weston," I teased.

Ben wished me a goodnight, and reluctantly, he left me.

He was nearly to the gate when I called out to him frantically. My emotions were still so overwhelming.

He stopped his horse, as I flew off the front porch, running barefoot across the yard toward him. He quickly dismounted and rushed to me, taking me in his arms. "Valynn, what is it?" he asked concerned.

I shook my head embarrassed, but I was so afraid for him to leave. "Tell me we really will marry tomorrow night, Ben! That nothing else is going to happen to keep us apart," I pleaded desperately.

Ben smiled tenderly and kissed me until I was certain that he wouldn't let anything come between us and Sherriff Byler.

He lifted me into his arms and carried me back onto the front porch, shaking his head at seeing I was barefoot.

I lay my head on his shoulder, wishing we never had to say goodbye.

"Tonight is the last night I will ever leave you. Tomorrow night, we won't have to say goodbye, just goodnight, Sweetheart," he assured me.

"I love you, Ben Weston, so very much." I kissed him with all the love my heart held for him, and he finally pulled back breathless.

"Valynn, you are killing me," he whispered.

I blushed and allowed him to leave the porch.

He smiled and walked toward his horse once again. "Get on inside now, Sweetheart; can't have you taking sick again. I might have lied just a bit because I don't think I can wait a second past tomorrow night to marry you," he said, smiling so handsomely.

My heart soared with happiness as I waved goodbye and watched as he rode away. Tomorrow night, I would be his, and we would never have to say goodbye again. I closed my eyes and thanked God for sending me Ben Weston and pleaded with Him to allow our wedding to go off without a hitch. I was losing patience, and eloping was sounding better by the second.

My mother came and stood beside me, wrapping an afghan around my shoulders tenderly. "It is too cool out here for you, Valynn," she scolded tenderly.

I nodded as I shivered.

"Don't worry, Love, tomorrow night you will marry."

I sighed and smiled. "I won't rest easy until I have that ring on my finger," I admitted.

Mother laughed warmly and hugged me to her. "Ben loves you, very much, Valynn. Trust in God, and His plan. His timing is never off *but always just on time*," she whispered.

I thought of Mother's words long after I lay in bed with Augusta on one side of me and Genevieve on the other. I didn't pretend to understand God's plan and why Niall had done what he did, but I did know my mother was right. If God allowed it to happen, there was a good reason behind it. No doubt it was to calm my impetuous nature. I might not ever know the reason. I could only pray, surrender my will to Him, and do my best to follow where He might lead me. I finally fell asleep with a new peace in my heart. Tomorrow night at this time, I would be Valynn Weston. And I could hardly wait!

"Beautiful dreamer, wake unto me, starlight and dew drops are waiting for thee." I heard angelic voices singing.

I struggled to open my eyes and smiled as I saw both my younger sisters standing beside my bed with a breakfast tray. "Breakfast in bed?" I asked, sitting up quickly. Excitement overwhelmed me, for today was the day! I looked toward the window, and the sun was up and shining beautifully, just as it should be.

"It is your last morning here with us at Andley Farms," Gen said emotionally.

I clasped a hand over my heart. She was right. I looked around my room wistfully; it was the last day I would wake to my lavender and pink floral wallpaper, my frilly pink curtains, and my sweet and yet wonderfully annoying sisters' faces. I fanned my face, fighting back my tears. What was it about falling in love that made you a bawling baby? I hated this part of it, and yet I wouldn't change a thing; I loved being in love with Ben Weston.

"Thank you, Angels," I whispered, pulling them both to me and kissing their cheeks.

"I made your favorite spiced muffins," Augusta said, teary eyed.

I thanked her. This was harder than I had imagined. I had been so very ready to leave home and marry for weeks now. I hadn't considered how hard it would be.

"Mother stayed up most of the night finishing your dress," Gen offered.

More tears. I shook my head; I would be lucky to get through this day without having red and puffy eyes.

"You really must stop being so sweet to me, or I shall cry all day," I said, wiping my eyes and cramming a muffin into my mouth.

Both of my sisters smiled. "You are much kinder since you fell in love with Ben," Augusta confessed.

I nearly laughed and nearly choked all at the same time, for she was most likely right. "There you go, say mean things to me, it is your last opportunity," I said, trying to gain control over my emotions.

"Girls, hurry now, we must be at Kenrick Farms just after lunch to help Georgie with Jori and the cooking," Mother called up to us.

I shooed them away lest they make me cry again. I ate my breakfast in bed, certain it was the last time I would get such a luxury. But I didn't care. I was ready to be a wife, Ben's wife. I shivered with giddiness and nearly wanted to squeal out loud. *I had never been so happy*.

I boiled water on the stove for my bath and soaked in the scented water. My mother made the loveliest soaps with rose petals, rosemary, and lemon oil. I washed my hair and tried to imagine doing these daily things in Ben's home, our home.

My sisters rolled my hair up in rags, and I allowed it to dry as they helped me finish my packing. They serenaded me with songs of love, both of them wistful and both anticipating their own futures and the dreams and hopes of falling in love. It was bittersweet listening to them dream out loud and knowing I would miss them so very much once I married. They danced around my room excitedly, and I had to laugh at their silliness. I adored them so.

"Valynn, we are going on over to Georgie's! Father will bring you on over this evening," Mother called up to me.

I rushed to the top of the stairs, panicked. I didn't want to be left alone. I truly hated being alone. "Wait for me, I am coming!" I said, rushing to my room and throwing on an old dress. I would get ready at Kenrick Farms. I had no desire to be alone all afternoon.

"Valynn! What if Ben is there, helping Keane?" Mother asked in frustration.

I laughed. "Then he shall see me in rag curlers! Please Mother, I don't want to be alone. I need to be around my sisters. I need the diversion," I pleaded.

She huffed and then smiled. "Hurry up then!" she urged.

I gathered up my wedding dress and shoes and rushed downstairs after them, singing the same silly love songs my sisters had earlier. I nearly jumped into the carriage and smiled. "Isn't it the most beautiful day ever?"

My mother and sisters smiled and chimed in with my singing as we made our way over to Kenrick Farms. I had never been so happy.

"Oh, my goodness! Ben is here!" I said, falling to the floor of the carriage and ducking my head.

Augusta and Genevieve burst into laughter, calling attention to our arrival.

"Good afternoon, Mrs. Andley, Girls," I heard him greet.

I smiled, for he had a most pleasant voice.

"Good afternoon, Ben!" my mother called out, amused.

"How was Valynn this morning, Mrs. Andley?" he asked.

I heard the concern in his voice. The sweet man was just as anxious as I was. *I loved him so.*

"She is blissfully happy, Ben. And is hiding in the carriage. Could you go into the barn and let her into the house? It is bad luck to see the bride before the wedding," my mother said. I could hear the happiness in her voice. She loved Ben.

"She is in there?" Ben asked, his voice coming closer.

Both of my sisters called out for him to stop.

"Valynn?" he called out sweetly.

I had to laugh. These next few hours would be the longest of my life I was certain. "Yes, Ben?" I called out.

I heard his sigh of relief. "I love you, Valynn," he said tenderly.

I blushed and felt near tears again. "I love you, too, Ben! Now scat! I can't stay hidden down here much longer," I laughed.

He laughed warmly. "All right, Sweetheart!" he said, leaving.

I heard Keane and Ben's brother Drew laughing and teasing him about being whipped and lassoed for life.

"Hey, Valynn!" Keane yelled out.

I shook my head. Men! "Yes, Keane?" I called out.

"Did Ben tell you what he was doing his last day as a bachelor?" my brother-in-law asked.

I sighed. "No, he didn't! What is he doing?" I asked, smiling. More than likely he was helping get ready for the reception in the barn.

"He's going to ride Ed Felter's crazed bull!"

I gasped, and my head shot up above the seat. Ed Felter's bull had caused numerous idiots in Crawford to be laid up for months, healing from their injuries. Some were nearly killed. "Keane Kenrick, you tell him right now, that he is not to get on that bull!" I said, jumping to my feet and bursting out the door of the carriage.

"Oh heavens, here we go," my mother said before praying out loud.

Keane and Drew stood smiling with their arms crossed. "I can't do that, Valynn. It's a man's right to spend his last hours of bachelorhood the way he wishes."

My temper flared. Of all the stupid things! "Keane! I am warning you!" I called out.

He simply laughed.

"Drew Weston! Talk some sense into him! This instant!" I said, stomping my foot hard on the dirt.

Drew shook his head and laughed.

I marched toward them, seeing red before my eyes.

"Valynn Clarice Andley, get back here before Ben sees you!" my mother warned.

But I would not listen. I would in no way let the man I loved ride a beast that was intent to kill, mere hours before our wedding. "Ben Weston! Get yourself out here!" I called angrily.

Keane held his hands up to stop me from going any farther. "Come now, Valynn, surely you don't...," I stopped him by shoving him hard, and he fell backwards into the horse trough.

"Valynn!" my mother screamed.

Drew burst into laughter just as Ben flew out of the barn. With one look at my hair up in rags, my anger flaring, and Keane in the horse trough, he burst into laughter.

I stomped my foot again. "Don't you dare get on that bull, Ben Weston! If you want beat up that badly, come here!" I said ready to fight someone.

"Valynn, Sweetheart, they are just teasing you," he said through his laughter.

Drew laughed even harder now. I was furious. How dare they tease me like that, on my wedding day? Keane was laughing as he pulled himself out of the trough.

My mother was beside me, trying to pull me toward the house.

I growled loudly and shoved Drew into the trough. "Very funny, Boys!" I hissed as I marched toward the house.

"Valynn, Sweetheart, come here," Ben called to me, still laughing.

I whirled around angry, tears stinging my eyes.

"No! Ben, turn around now, you're not supposed to see her. Valynn, come inside!" my mother said, growing as angry as I was.

"Good luck with that one, Ben," I heard Keane say. He stood dripping wet and shaking his head in disbelief.

I started marching back toward them, certain they hadn't learned a thing. Drew took off running, wet, into the barn; Keane was on his heels, laughing. "That's right, Boys! See where teasing me like that again gets you!" I said, nearly to cry. *Immature idiots*!

"Valynn, come here, Sweetheart," Ben laughed, pulling me closely.

I felt my hot and angry tears on my cheeks. Ben searched my face, trying his best not to laugh. "You're a pain in the backside, Ben Weston!" I said.

He smiled and kissed me soundly. "And you are even more beautiful when you're all riled up and angry," he whispered.

My heart raced and I kissed him again.

My mother yanked the back of my dress, pulling me away.

I had to laugh as she swatted my behind and urged me into the farmhouse. I paused at the door, looking to find Ben still watching. I blew him a kiss, and he smiled and shook his head. "If I even hear of you going near that bull, Ben Weston!" I warned coyly. But I was quite serious.

He held his hands innocently up in the air as he laughed.

I walked into the house with a small amount of satisfaction.

I stood before the long oval mirror in the guest room where I stayed when coming to Kenrick Farms.

"Oh, Val," Georgie whispered emotionally.

"She looks like a vision," Celia said teary eyed.

I turned to my mother, and she nodded, too overcome with emotion to speak. I ran into her arms and hugged her. Then I hugged each of my four sisters at least twice.

"You look beautiful, Valynn," Genevieve said wistfully.

I thanked her as a knock sounded at the door.

My mother squeezed my shoulders tenderly. "It is time, Baby," she whispered.

I nodded, for I was ready. She shook her head and smiled through fresh tears.

"You have made a wise choice, Valynn. You and Ben will have a blessed life," she whispered.

I nodded again, too emotional to speak, for I truly believed we would.

My father poked his head inside and the tender look on his face was nearly my undoing.

"If anyone else says something sappy to me!" I warned, fanning my face, willing back my tears.

My mother ushered my sisters downstairs and smiled as she left my father alone with me.

"Oh, my Val," father said tenderly.

I sighed and smiled through my tears. It was no use, I was a bawl bag.

"You look lovely, Val," he whispered.

I thanked him, and he hugged me closely. I sniffed in his smell of peppermint and tobacco and smiled.

"I guess it is just about time to give another one of my girls away. Ben is a fine man, Val. I am proud of your choice. You will have a good life at Weston Farms. And I am thankful," he said emotionally.

I kissed his cheek. "Thank you, Father. I love you," I whispered.

"I love you, my Val," he whispered, his eyes glistening with unshed tears.

I could only pray he waited to do his crying away from me. The piano music began to play downstairs in the parlor, and I took my father's arm and smiled.

"Ready?" he asked as my sister Augusta's angelic voice filled the air.

I nodded. "I am past ready," I admitted, giggling in nerves and excitement.

My father patted my hand tenderly and we began our decent downstairs. My heart raced wildly.

My father paused at the door of the parlor, and I looked around the small room, crowded with people who loved me, who loved Ben. Loved ones who would support us in prayer, who would lend a hand to help us in days to come, and who would share in each joy and each sorrow life brought our way. I smiled brightly, for I couldn't ask for more than this.

Ben stood next to Sheriff Byler in a new grey suit and bow tie, looking incredibly handsome. Our eyes met, Ben's twinkling with love for me. My eyes never left his as I slowly made my way toward him, ready to join my life to his, forever.

My father gave my hand to Ben, and Ben lifted it tenderly and placed a kiss on my knuckles.

"Not yet, Son," Sheriff Byler teased.

Everyone chuckled, and I felt my face warm in a blush.

Ben merely smiled.

I listened to Ben as he promised his life to me to love, to cherish, to uphold, and to protect. I had no doubts about this man, none. I smiled as he slid a dainty golden band onto my finger, claiming me for his own. I could have kissed him right then and there.

I pledged to him my life, vowed to keep him in sickness, in health, in lean, and in gain. And I couldn't help but smile as I caught glimpses of that boy so many years ago, in the face of the wonderful man before me now.

"You may now kiss your bride, Son," Sheriff Byler said, smiling.

Ben pulled me into a passionate kiss that had the room in an uproar of laughter and cheers. He pressed his forehead to mine tenderly. "We did it," he whispered.

I clung to him, never wishing to let go. "Thank you, God in heaven," I whispered emotionally.

Ben nodded. "I have every second, since your father placed your hand in mine."

I kissed him again, tears streaming down my cheeks, my heart so full of love for him.

"Come on you two, there's time enough for that later. It's time for cake!" Keane said, laughing.

I let go of Ben, frowning, and put my hands on my hips.

Keane's eyes grew as big as saucers and he quickly fled the room, leaving us alone.

Ben laughed and hugged me to him.

"Do we have to stay for dancing?" he asked softly.

I nodded through my blush, feeling shy suddenly. "At least for a little while," I whispered.

Ben smiled, and we walked arm and arm to where everyone had gathered into the barn for our reception. The barn was lit with dozens of lanterns, and music had started to play. Everyone clapped as we entered, and I gasped in shock and covered my mouth with my hands as I burst into laughter at the sight of our wedding cake.

"Valynn!" Ben scolded.

I couldn't stop laughing. "I had nothing to do with it!" I insisted, but I could see he didn't believe me.

He smiled but shook his head in frustration. Before us stood a lovely three tiered wedding cake, trimmed in green ribbon, and two porcelain frogs dressed as a bride and groom as the cake topper. A homemade banner draped behind the refreshment table and read, "*She's got you now, Frog Ben.*"

I couldn't stop laughing. I lay my head on Ben's chest as he growled. I hugged him tightly. "They are right, you know? I have you, and I will never let you go, *my Frog Ben!*"

As Ben hugged me closely and led me in a waltz, I watched as our family and friends smiled and laughed as they danced and celebrated our marriage along with us.

I closed my eyes and thanked God for leading me to Ben, for guiding us every step of the way, and for blessing me with a Godly husband- a man who had fasted, who had prayed for this very day for over a year.

God had blessed us with a love so pure and true, and I would spend the rest of my life thanking *Him* for each day He allowed me to spend with Ben, *my husband, my life, and always, my Frog Ben.*

The End.

TO MY READERS

I hope you have enjoyed reading *Valynn*, Book Two of The Andley Sisters Series. Be looking for the next two books in this series coming soon! Also being released in the fall of 2016 is *Estelle*, Book One in The Royals of Gliston Series. Your feedback is very important to me. Please find me on Goodreads, Amazon, or from one of the social media links below, and leave me a comment.

Be blessed,

Sherri Beth Johnson

Watch the book trailer to The Andley Sisters Series for *Georgiana* and *Valynn* at https://youtu.be/VApSsx8ECzc

Website: www.sherribethjohnson.wordpress.com

Email: sherribethjohnson@gmail.com

Facebook: www.facebook.com/sherribethjohnson

Instagram: sbethjohnson41

Twitter: @sbethjohnson

Pinterest: sbjAuthor

35171373R00125

Made in the USA
Middletown, DE
21 September 2016